"I was doing just fine until you dropped in!"

Ross's voice was savage as he pulled the car to the side of the road.

"You mean, you'd driven it under," Nicola responded softly and soothingly. "You didn't kill her, Ross, and you can't spend the rest of your life shutting yourself away because some people who don't know you think you did."

Ross's eyes searched her face intently. "You don't know me at all. What makes you so sure I was telling the truth?"

"I suppose you'd have to call it a gut feeling," Nicola answered slowly, watching Ross's expression change from hostile to vulnerable to passionate as he suddenly reached for her.

"You should have let me take you back to Caracas," he said thickly.

"No," Nicola whispered, "not until you can tell me with honesty that you don't want me here."

"I can't do that."

KAY THORPE, an English author, has always been able to spin a good yarn. In fact, her teachers said she was the best storyteller in the school—particularly with excuses for being late! Kay then explored a few unsatisfactory career paths before giving rein to her imagination and hitting the jackpot with her first romance novel. After a roundabout route, she'd found her niche at last. The author is married with one son.

Books by Kay Thorpe

HARLEQUIN PRESENTS
822—DOUBLE DECEPTION
853—SOUTH SEAS AFFAIR
902—DANGEROUS MOONLIGHT
941—WIN OR LOSE
973—JUNGLE ISLAND
1084—TIME OUT OF MIND

HARLEQUIN ROMANCE
2232—THE WILDERNESS TRAIL
2234—FULL CIRCLE

Don't miss any of our special offers. Write to us at the following address for information on our newest releases.

Harlequin Reader Service
901 Fuhrmann Blvd., P.O. Box 1397, Buffalo, NY 14240
Canadian address: P.O. Box 603,
Fort Erie, Ont. L2A 5X3

KAY THORPE

land of illusion

Harlequin Books

TORONTO • NEW YORK • LONDON
AMSTERDAM • PARIS • SYDNEY • HAMBURG
STOCKHOLM • ATHENS • TOKYO • MILAN

Harlequin Presents first edition January 1989
ISBN 0-373-11141-X

Original hardcover edition published in 1988
by Mills & Boon Limited

Printed in U.S.A.

CHAPTER ONE

THEY would know she was gone by now. Stumbling along the narrow dirt road, clothing plastered to her body by the teeming rain, Nicola fought to contain the fear mounting inside her as the light swiftly faded. She had gambled on reaching the small township through which they had passed earlier, but it was proving further than she had thought. The idea of spending the night in the open was daunting, yet rather the Venezuelan wildlife than the plans those two back there had for her!

The sound of an engine brought her heart into her mouth before she realised it was coming towards her, not after her. Headlights cut twin swathes through the rain as the vehicle rounded the bend up ahead. Frantically, she waved both arms, light-headed with relief when the Land Rover screeched to a halt.

There was a clearly audible curse from within, and a head was thrust through the open window.

'What the hell do you think you're doing?' demanded a rough-toned male voice.

'I need help,' Nicola said urgently, hoping she wasn't jumping from the frying-pan into the fire. 'There are two men after me!'

The head was withdrawn, the passenger door shoved open. 'You'd better get in.'

She did so gratefully, slumping into the bucket seat with a quivery exhalation of pent-up breath. It was already too dark to see much of her rescuer. She had a vague impression of hard-boned features and black hair. 'Thanks,' she got out. 'You just saved my life!'

Dark brows lifted a fraction as he studied her. 'They're out to kill you?'

'Or worse.' A shudder ran through her at the thought of what would have happened had she not seized her chance to get away. 'Can you take me to the town back there?' she asked. 'It can't be far.'

He made no immediate move. 'You've got friends in Santa Elena?'

'No,' she admitted. 'I don't know anyone in Venezuela. It's the only place I *can* go for the moment.'

He seemed to come to some swift decision, reaching out to thrust the gear lever into first. 'I doubt if you'd find much security back there. I live a few miles away. You'll be safer.'

'I can't impose . . .' she began automatically, her voice fading into silence as he slanted an ironical glance.

'True-blue British,' he observed. 'You'd sooner I left you to fend for yourself?'

'No.' She gave a wry little laugh. 'I suppose that did sound stupid, considering.'

'Very,' he agreed drily. 'Anyway, I'd be interested to hear what a girl like you is doing way out here on her own in the first place.'

Nicola sighed. 'It's a long story.'

'It will take us twenty minutes to get where we're going, in this,' he returned. 'I can listen while I drive. Fire away.'

It was her turn to slant a glance. 'You're American, aren't you?'

'Every inch.' There was a pause before he added,

'You're evading the issue.'

'Not really,' she acknowledged. 'Just gathering myself together. It's been pretty much shock on shock these past couple of days.' She drew a sharp breath as headlights sprang into view ahead. 'It's them! It has to be!'

'OK,' he said. 'Get down out of sight until we're past.'

Nicola did so, her heart thudding as the other vehicle slowed on approach. There was a terrifying moment when she thought some challenge was going to be made, then the engine note altered again, picking up speed as the truck pulled away.

'You can get up now,' advised her rescuer. 'They've gone.'

'It was an effort to raise herself upright. Nicola hadn't realised just how exhausted she was. The hands gripping the sides of the seat showed white at the knuckles.

'Thanks,' she said again. 'Do you think they'll come back when they don't find me further along the road?'

'If they do, we're not going to be here,' came the reasonable and comforting reply. 'And unless they know the district pretty well they're unlikely to strumble on El Milagro—especially in the rain.'

'That's the name of your house?'

'*Rancho*,' he corrected. 'It belongs to a friend.' This time the pause was lengthier. 'Feeling up to it yet?'

She wasn't feeling up to anything much, but it had to be gone through. Sitting back, trying to relax taut nerves, she said jerkily, 'They promised me a lift back to Caracas. I didn't have any other choice.'

'There's always a choice,' he said. 'Like yes and no, for instance. And suppose you start at the beginning. A name might help.'

'Nicola Sanderson.' She made another uncertain little gesture. It's difficult to know where to start. I arrived in Velida expecting to find the Crossmans waiting for me, only they weren't there. They'd only provided a one-way ticket, and I didn't have enough money of my own to get back to the coast, I . . .'

'Hardly the beginning,' came the dry interruption. 'Give me the whole scenario, from day one.'

Collecting her thoughts was difficult. Nicola tried to cast her mind back to the world she had left those three long days ago. 'I answered an advert for an English nanny to look after a six-year-old boy for a year,' she said at length. 'I was out of work and rather desperate, you see. The salary sounded excellent, and a year isn't so long. I thought it might give me a breathing space.'

'You're a qualified children's nurse?'

'No,' Nicola admitted, and then, on a faintly defensive note, 'As a matter of fact, I'm an actress.'

He shot her another of those swift, appraising glances. 'Anyone I should have heard of?'

'Not unless you happened to catch the play I had a bit part in'. She was too weary to be bitter. 'It folded out of town. I don't suppose you've any idea just how many drama school graduates there are looking for work?'

'I could take an educated guess.' He was silent for a moment. 'So you took the first job you could find?'

'More or less. Qualifications were unnecessary, it said. Applicants had to be English, and capable of teaching a six-year-old the basics, that was all.'

'You were interviewed?'

'By the agency handling the job.' Nicola shrugged. 'I was lucky—if you can call it that. It seemed there were very few people willing to spend a year in a place as remote as Velida. I was offered the post almost immediately.'

'It never occurred to you to check the details with any authority before leaving England?'

She shook her head. 'Everything seemed very much above board. They even showed me a photograph of the family I'd be living with.'

'English themselves?'

'So they said. He—Mr Crossman, I mean— managed a cacao plantation. They'd been out here for seven years. My air fare was paid through to Caracas.'

'That's more than a hundred miles away.'

'I know. I expected some kind of transport to have been arranged, but the local buses were cheap enough.'

He shook his own head as if in disbelief. 'Didn't you suspect something wrong right then?'

Nicola bit her lip. 'I suppose I should have done, but I just assumed there'd been some mix-up over my arrival date. Anyway, I didn't have a return ticket.'

'You could have gone to the Consulate.'

'In retrospect, I could have done a whole lot of things'.

He accepted that without comment. She supposed there was little to add to what he had already intimated. She had been a fool. That went without saying, anyway. Only anyone could be wise after the event.

'So you put your trust in your two friends back there,' he prompted. 'Where did you meet them?'

'In a café,' she ackowledged. 'They looked decent enough.'

His laugh was short. 'Face values aren't worth a dime!'

'So I realised.' The tremors were starting again, down deep, at the memory. 'They said they knew where they could get a good price for a blonde-haired European. I didn't know that kind of thing still went on!'

'It still goes on. A white girl on her own must have seemed like manna from heaven to their kind.' He didn't look at her. 'Did they harm you?'

There was no doubting what he meant. 'No, thank God!'

'Unspoiled goods fetch a higher price. How did you manage to get away from them?'

'They stopped to make camp for the night and left me tied up in the back of the truck while they went hunting.'

'None too well, by the sound of it.'

'My wrists are very supple, and I was soaked in perspiration. I managed to wriggle free. I knew we'd passed through a small town a while back. I hoped I could reach it before they discovered I'd gone. If you hadn't come along when you did . . .' She broke off, swallowing painfully on the hardness in her throat. 'They still have all my things.'

'You've seen the last of those.'

'But my passport!'

'That might present a problem, but nothing that can't be fixed, given time and patience.' He trod on the brakes as some animal ran across the road in front of the car, swearing under his breath. 'First thing we have to do is get you to Caracas.'

Nicola looked at him swiftly. 'Tonight?'

'Hardly. There's no way I'm driving that distance at night in these conditions. I guess you'll just have to sit it out till morning.'

She waited a fraction too long before voicing the question. 'You're on your own?'

'Apart from the staff. Carlos went on a trip.' His

upper lip had a visible tilt. 'Don't worry, I'm not about to add to your problems. Right now, you need a bath and a change of clothes. Maria will find you something.'

Another woman. Reassurances withstanding, Nicola could only be thankful. She needed badly to sleep. It seemed an age since she had seen a bed. It had taken two days to reach Velida. Two days of bumpy, muddy roads, with the only chance of sleep a snatched couple of hours here and there in a village rest hut. And then the horror and despair of reaching her destination, to find herself abandoned. She had long since given up trying to work out what her employer had been thinking of. Obviously, it had not been of her. Since meeting up with Rodrigo and Juan she had run a whole new gamut of emotions. Right now, she felt drained.

'You didn't tell me who you are yet,' she murmured after a while.

Just for a moment he seemed to hesitate. 'The name's King,' he said. 'Ross King.'

Somewhere at the back of her mind a thought came and went, too fleeting to grasp. She said thickly, 'I owe you a lot, Mr King.'

'Glad to be of service.' He slowed the car, peering ahead through the streaming windscreen. 'There should be a turn-off about now. There it is! Hold tight. It's not much more than a track from here.'

He wasn't exaggerating. Around them the lush tropical forest crowded in, dank and odorous. The rainy season was supposed to be over, according to what Nicola had understood. Leaving England in the grip of a foggy November, she had anticipated blue skies and hot sun, but she had seen little enough of either so far. Once she got back home to England, she was staying there for sure!

When she got back. Right now, that seemed far distant. A new passport wasn't going to be obtained without cutting through a whole lot of red tape. Time and patience, Ross King had said. Which was all very well, only time meant money—somewhere to stay, food to eat, clothes to wear. She had nothing except for the slacks and shirt she stood up in; her lightweight pumps were mud-soaked beyond redemption.

They forded a river, the water already half-way up the axles. Nicola knew a momentary concern, swiftly swamped by the ever-increasing tiredness. The forest thinned, giving way to cleared ground. Lights showed ahead. They drove through a gateway and came to a halt before a single-storeyed building, fronted by a wide veranda.

Already soaked as she was, Nicola saw little point in hurrying to gain the shelter of the house. Ross himself paid scant attention to the rain as he led the way inside. The main doors gave access to a large living area, walled in white, roughcast plaster and furnished Spanish style with ornately carved chairs and tables, the tiled floor scattered with rugs. An archway led through to other regions. In this appeared an olive-skinned woman of indeterminate age, clad in a long black skirt and white peasant blouse.

She spoke in Spanish, her dark eyes appraising the newcomer as Ross apparently explained her presence in the same language. When he had finished, she held out a hand, her smile suggesting sympathy in any language.

'Come,' she said.

Ross nodded as Nicola glanced his way. 'Maria will

see you OK. We'll eat after you've dried off.'

Nicola would have preferred sleep to food, but she couldn't bring herself to say so. The temperature had dropped with the onset of darkness. She felt shivery—although that was as likely to be from reaction as chill.

Maria took her to a bathroom that had every convenience one might expect, if not exactly sumptous in its appointments. Turning on both taps of the large white bath, she indicated to Nicola to take off her sodden clothing, departing with the garments held at arm's length. Thick Turkish towels hung ready over a rail. Nicola turned off the taps when she judged the water deep enough, lowering herself into the comforting warmth with a sigh of sheer relief. There was a hand-shower attachment, too. She used it to wash and rinse her hair, content to settle for soap in lieu of shampoo. Cleanliness was next to Godliness, her mother had always said. It certainly beat smelly mud!

Maria returned, bearing an assortment of garments, while Nicola was drying herself, depositing them on the wooden stool with another smile and an encouraging nod.

There were no underclothes, Nicola realised on sorting through the things after the woman had departed again. She settled in the end on a pair of white cotton trousers and shirt which must belong to a boy, as they fitted her slender shape without undue tucking and pulling in. A pair of espadrilles only a size or so too large completed her outfit. If she shuffled, they might stay on. Her face looked drawn in the damp-spotted mirror, blue eyes darkened by fatigue. But she was safe. That was what counted. She had escaped the ultimate horror by the skin of her teeth.

Ross was waiting for her in the living-room. He had changed his beige bush shirt for another of the same style in white, she noted. He was even taller than she had first imagined, broad of shoulder and lean of hip. Grey eyes held a speculative expression as he took in the drying cloud of pale gold hair.

'Better,' he approved. 'Less of the drowned rat!'

He was deliberately lightening the atmosphere, Nicola realised, catching the inflection. The happenings of the last two days could not and would not be easily forgotten, but they were already receding from the forefront of her mind. Looking now at the lean, intelligent features, she felt a tingle of awareness along her spine. Attractive—no, more than that, arresting—that was Ross King. The name seemed somehow familiar, yet she could conjure no memory of having heard it before. How could she have, anyway?

'Maria is bringing supper through here,' he said 'Hope you like *paella*?'

'I don't mind what I eat,' Nicola told him, adding diffidently, 'Actually, I'm not all that hungry.'

'They fed you?'

'No,' she admitted. 'I couldn't have stomached it then, either.'

'Reaction,' he stated. 'You need something on your stomach, if only to stop it playing you up later. Fancy a brandy?'

She grimaced. 'Not right now.'

'Later, then. It will help you sleep.'

Short of that commodity though she was, the immediate urge seemed to have faded. At his invitation, she settled herself in one of the big cushioned chairs, watching him as he took a seat opposite. He seemed so much at home here, yet he had stated himself that the place didn't belong to him. Carlos was away on a trip, he had said. Who Carlos was still had to be ascertained.

'Have you been here long?' she asked. 'At El Milagro, I mean.'

'Some months.' The grey eyes had acquired a sudden shuttered look—like a steel curtain coming down. 'We're going to need a plan of campaign if we're to get you back to where you belong. First thing in the morning, we'll drive into Santa Elena and report the abduction. They're unlikely to catch those two now, but at least we can try. You'll need something in the way of clothing, too. Those things are hardly fit for a visit to the Consulate.'

'My own things should be all right after they're washed,' Nicola responded. 'I've already put you to a lot of trouble.'

'Suggest an alternative,' he invited with an edge of irony. 'You might be all kinds of a fool for coming here, but you didn't choose to be landed in this mess. If I had a daughter your age, I'd like to think somebody would do the same for her.'

Nicola's smile was involuntary. 'If you had a daughter my age, you'd need to be a lot older than you look!'

One eyebrow rose. 'And how old do I look?'

She shrugged, sensing ridicule. 'Thirty-five, perhaps.'

'I'm thirty-nine,' he acknowledged drily. 'That gives me a good twenty years' seniority, I'd say.'

'Eighteen, actually.'

'Sure.' He sounded sceptical. 'What did your family have to say about this wonderful job of yours? Or didn't you bother telling them?

Something inside her closed up. 'My mother died a year ago. I never knew my father. Illegitimate is the polite word.'

'Stop feeling sorry for yourself,' he came back hardily. 'There are plenty of others in the same boat.'

She gave a faithful imitation of his own sardonic lip slant. 'You included?'

His grin was as sudden a it was unexpected. 'Quick on the draw, aren't you, honey?'

'Firing as I go,' she agreed wryly, already regretting the retort. 'I suppose I am pretty sensitive about it.'

'Only you feel the need to get it out in the open soonest.'

She hadn't thought of it that way, but he was right, she was forced to admit. Tell the truth and shame the devil, as her mother had so often said. She had been full of advice like that. Making up for the one great sin she had committed, Nicola supposed now with sudden insight. Having a daughter eager to make a career of the stage couldn't have been easy for her to accept, yet she had moved heaven and earth to provide the wherewithal to help her through drama school.

'I'm a bundle of neuroses,' she claimed with assumed lightness. 'That's only one of them!'

'You wouldn't know a neurosis if it ran over you,' he scoffed. 'Quit dramatising. I'm not impressed.'

She eyed him sourly. 'I expect it takes a whole lot to impress you, Mr King.'

'Some,' he agreed, unmoved by the sarcasm.

Maria arrived bearing a loaded tray which she set down on the lower table close by. 'Eat,' she commanded.

The *paella* was delicious, Nicola had to concede.

Despite her protestations, she found herself finishing every morsel.

'Recovery is fast at your age,' Ross observed, watching as she chased the last grain of rice around the plate with a fingertip. 'There's more if you want it.'

She shook her head, her smile spontaneous. 'Enough is enough. I'm fit to burst already.'

'You don't look it.' There was nothing particularly complimentary in his inflection, he was simply stating a fact. 'Think you might sleep without nightmares?'

Nicola hid an involuntary shudder. 'I can but try.'

'The brandy might help.' He was moving as he spoke, crossing to a carved cabinet to take out bottle and glasses. 'One small one, and then bed.'

She said sharply, 'I'm not a child!'

'That's true.' He didn't turn. 'You'd rather I took you to bed than sent you, maybe?'

'Don't be ridiculous!' She was doing this all wrong and she knew it, yet some perverse instinct refused to let go.

'Hardly ridiculous. You're female, I'm male. That's all it takes.'

He was laughing at her, Nicola thought painfully, and she had asked for it. What had got into her, acting this way?

'I'm sorry,' she said on a subdued note. 'I'm the one who's being ridiculous.'

'You're under strain.' Ross brought across the brandy, placing the glass on the table at her side. It was difficult to tell what he was thinking at that moment. He was obviously a past master of the inscrutable expression. 'Things will look better in the morning. They always do.'

He was saying that in the manner of one offering reassurance, rather than with any great belief, Nicola reflected fleetingly. Nothing would have changed in the morning. She would still be in the same mess. Yet, with Ross King to help smooth the way, it might not be too bad. She had to put her faith in someone.

'You're very kind,' she murmured, and saw his lips twist.

'It depends on the viewpoint. Short of keeping you here, I don't have much choice.'

'Some might have simply put me on a bus back to Caracas and left it at that,' she pointed out. 'After all, if I'm capable of getting this far on my own, I'm capable of getting back.'

'Always providing you didn't run into any more helpful characters on the way.' He made a dismissive gesture. 'Drink your brandy. I'll get Maria to show your room.'

The Venezuelan woman came at once to his call. Nicola had the feeling she might have been hovering somewhere close, in order to appraise the situation. Perhaps there had been other females here before her, if in somewhat different circumstances. Ross didn't give the impression of being a complete recluse.

He was drinking whisky when she took her leave. She wondered if it was a nightly ritual. His presence out here in the wilderness of the Venezuelan jungle was a puzzle in itself. A man of purpose, she would have thought, yet there could be little of it in this neck of the woods. Perhaps he was hiding from something —or someone. Not that he looked the criminal type, either—if there was such a thing. Tomorrow, she might even ask him. He could only tell her to mind her own business.

The room to which Maria took her had the same functional appearance as the rest of the house. Whoever this Carlos was, he lived a fairly simple lifestyle. A voluminous nightdress of plain white cotton was spread ready across the bed. One of Maria's own, Nicola gathered from the former's beaming pantomime. Regarding herself in the mirror after donning it, she felt hysterical laughter welling up inside. No man seeing her in this shapeless *tent* would find himself remotely tempted. She looked like some waif and stray!

At least the bed was comfortable. Lying there between thin cotton sheets listening to the rain still teeming down, she tried to switch off her mind, without success. Even if and when she eventually got back to England, there was going to be little enough there for her. She had given up the bedsit she had called home on leaving the country, and would have a hard time finding anywhere else to live with no job to go to. Why, oh, why hadn't she stayed where she was, safe and at least reasonably secure? This job had been too good to be true, anyway. She should have known that. Viewed in retrospect, the entire happenings of the past few days were almost unbelievable—like something out of a book, or a film. In fact, it would have to be a great director who could make her situation seem feasible, even on camera.

It was there and then that it came to her at last, bringing her sharply upright in the narrow bed. Ross King! No wonder the name had seemed familiar! Little more than a year ago it had been on all the placards, his photograph plastered across double columns.

The newspaper account had made little lasting impression at the time, it was true. The kind of people it had been written about lived lives far outside the normal sphere. The headline came back to her with clarity now: 'Film Director Suspected of Wife Killing'. It had caught her eye mainly because she had shortly before seen a film directed by Ross King; the last in a line of three that had made his wife into a star.

Arlene Carol had been a complete unknown before her marriage, yet within months of it had shot to overnight fame with the leading role in a film that had owed the greater part of its success to the superb direction. Nicola remembered her as a strikingly beautiful brunette who projected a sensuality that seemed to reach right out from the screen to embrace every male in the cinema audience—or so she had gathered from those whose opinions on the subject had been imparted to her. Death had cut short that career on a Californian road when her car had gone over a cliff. Within hours, Ross King had been in custody with a first-degree murder charge hanging over his head—charges later dropped due to lack of conclusive evidence, although too late to stop the media from making free with his marital problems. His wife's passions had not, it seemed, been confined solely to himself and to the screen. Her affairs with other men had been breaking up the marriage long before her death. As he himself had been reported as saying, if he'd been going to kill her at all, he would have done it the first time. But the mud had stuck. Many, it seemed, had believed him guilty.

Did she? Nicola asked herself now, hugging her knees as she gazed into the darkness. She could visualise those strong, vital features in her mind's eye. He didn't look like a murderer, but then who could tell what a man might be driven to under certain circumstances—or a woman either, if it came to that? If his wife's death was the reason he had shut himself off from the world this way, he must have loved her a great deal. Certainly he had made no films since. But what a waste of a talent such as his! The hottest property in Hollywood, they had called him.

Considering that by this time tomorrow she would have said goodbye to him anyway, she supposed it scarcely mattered what she believed. If the truth were known, the thought of leaving here held little appeal. In Carcacas she would be on her own again, dependent on the slow-turning wheels of officialdom. Whatever sum was loaned her in order to get her home again, she would be expected to pay it back, which meant that, even if she did manage to find a job of some kind, the debt would be a millstone round her neck for a long time to come. Yet what other way was there?

CHAPTER TWO

THINGS will look better in the morning, Ross King had said. Gazing from her bedroom window at the broad expanse of water spreading out from the overflowing river, Nicola thought wryly that the prophecy had been somewhat optimistic. The house itself was built on slightly higher ground, so it seemed safe enough for the present. Judging from the foliage still protruding above the surface of the new lake, the depth wasn't all that great as yet. Whether it would remain that way, with the rain still coming down in stair-rods, was something else again. If she was going to get away from this place at all, it needed to be fairly soon.

Dressed in the same shirt and trousers she had worn the night before, she went in search of her benefactor. Ross was drinking coffee out on the veranda, viewing the flood with unthrilled eyes.

'Could be worse,' he observed in answer to Nicola's query. 'The car's out, I guess, but we might get through to Santa Elena on horseback.'

'I don't ride,' she said nervously, and received a brief glance.

'So we'll tie you on and use a leading rein. Maria's fixing you some breakfast. The coffee's fresh, if you want to pour yourself a cup.'

He was different this morning, Nicola reflected, complying with the suggestion: more brittle. The weather? Or was it simply her presence here that was disturbing him? Most likely a combination of the two.

Knowing who he was made her own position difficult. She felt constrained, unsure whether to bring the subject out into the open or leave well alone. For the present, she opted for the latter course.

'Does this sort of thing happen often?' she asked.

'Only in the rainy season,' came the dry reply.

'I thought that finished in October.'

'It's not an overnight switch-off, although I guess it is going on a bit longer than usual this year.'

'Just my luck.' She tried to keep the comment light. 'Do you think the roads back to Caracas will be open?'

'That's what we're going to find out, once we've eaten. I told Maria to prepare ham and eggs for both of us. OK?'

Nicola's laugh sounded false even to her own ears. 'Sounds good. Not what I'd have expected way out here in the jungle, though!'

'Carlos keeps pigs and cures his own,' said Ross. 'Hens, too. With goats for milk, and a variety of crops to draw on, he's pretty self-sufficient so far as food is concerned.'

'He's a farmer, then?'

Grey eyes retained their present outlook over the flooded landscape. 'He's a man who prefers his own company.'

'Except for you,' she ventured, and saw broad shoulders lift in a brief shrug.

'We respect each other's privacy.'

Perhaps this Carlos, too, had a past, Nicola reflected, and found herself wondering once more about that of the man seated opposite her at the plain deal table. No matter what the burden carried, shutting oneself away from the civilised world was surely not the best way to handle it? She stole a

glance at the firm profile, dwelling for a fleeting
moment or two on hard male cheekbones and clean-
cut jawline. His nose was thin, almost aquiline, his
mouth cynical in repose. A man who had seen too
much of everything; a man who quickened her pulses
with his very presence. Physical attraction took little
note of who or what a person was, that much she
already knew. Ross King stirred something in her
that she'd rarely experienced before.

'You're safe enough,' he said with irony into the
silence. 'Even if I'd been tried and convicted, it
wouldn't necessarily make me a homicidal maniac.'

The directness of the attack momentarily stunned
her. It was the last thing she had been expecting.
'I don't know what you're talking about,' she
floundered. 'What on earth . . .'

'Don't take me for a complete fool.' His glance was
derisive. 'You've been watching me as if I'd sprouted
two heads since the minute you came on the scene!'

'Perhaps I was simply admiring the one,' she
retorted, rallying with an effort. 'After all, you're an
attractive man, Mr King.'

He made an impatient gesture. 'Do me a favour
and stop playing games. The name meant something
to you last night, only you were too tired to realise
why.'

There was no point in further denial, Nicola had to
acknowledge. She tried to look him straight in the
eye. 'All right, so I know who you are. There's no
need to get paranoid about it.'

He looked at her for a long, still moment, eyes
narrowed, then his mouth relaxed suddenly into a
faint smile. 'You're right, that's what I am. I thought
I was over it. Just goes to show.'

'I'm sorry,' she ventured. 'I wasn't sure whether to say anything or not. I only realised after I'd gone to bed last night.'

'Did it keep you awake?'

'Not so as you'd notice. As you said, I was tired.'

'With reason.' There was a pause; his expression was under control again. 'How much *do* you know exactly?'

'Only what was reported in the newspapers at the time.' She attempted the same unemotional delivery. 'One newspaper, that was. There was a photograph of you—and your wife.'

'The wife I was suspected of killing.'

'Yes.' It was almost a relief to hear him say it. 'But you were cleared.'

'That's right, I was cleared. But neither soon enough nor well enough to convince you, apparently.'

Her head snapped up. 'I didn't say that!'

'You don't have to say it. I've long learned to recognise that look.'

She said softly, 'Is that why you're here in this place?'

'Part of it, maybe.' Ross shook his head. 'Let's forget it. We'll be in Santa Elena in a couple of hours, and hopefully on the way north soon after that.'

Nicola looked down at her cup. 'You'll come back to El Milagro after you drop me in Caracas?'

'Sure.'

'To spend another year in isolation? I can't see how that will help.'

'You don't understand the situation,' he said. 'You can't be expected to.'

But she could, Nicola thought. Knowing the facts, she could well understand. What she couldn't do was condone this kind of existence as a solution. Turning one's back on a problem didn't make it go away.

There seemed little she could say, and certainly nothing that he might listen to. One didn't go interfering in someone else's private affairs.

Maria brought the food. Fried in olive oil, the ham and eggs were too greasy for Nicola's taste. She had to force herself to eat a fair portion.

'I'm not as hungry as I thought,' she excused herself, catching Ross's eye as she pushed away her plate.

'There's no penalty.' He sounded indifferent. 'If you're ready, we'll make a start.'

It had at last stopped raining, Nicola saw in relief. Not that it was going to be a dry journey, by any means. Wading through floods on horseback sounded hazardous. Yet, even if the rain held off, it might be days before the water went down. Days which Ross King was obviously not prepared to wait. He wanted her out now.

Her own clothing had been washed and ironed, her shoes rendered wearable again, if badly stained. At Ross's suggestion, a plastic-wrapped package was made of all items, so that she would have something dry to change into when they reached Santa Elena. Tied on with string, the espadrilles would suffice for now, providing she wasn't called upon to walk very far.

The horses were stabled across a dirt-floored yard: big, powerful animals both. Used for pulling ploughs as well as carrying people, Nicola judged, eyeing the pair of them in trepidation.

A small, wiry man, dressed much as she was herself, held them in check with a hand on each set of reins. Nicola wondered if he was the one whose clothes she was wearing. She attempted to ask him, only to be met with a blank, uncomprehending stare.

'They're his son's,' Ross replied. 'Ramón is Maria's husband.'

An incongruous match, she reflected. Maria was twice his size!

Ross gave her a leg up on to one broad back. Easing herself gingerly down into the saddle, Nicola was grateful for the horns fore and aft to which she could cling. No attempt was made to fasten her into her seat. He simply clipped on a length of rope, the free end of which he kept in his hand as he swung himself astride the other animal. The package containing all she had left in the world was strapped across the back of his straddle. Ross himself looked perfectly at home on horseback.

They left without ceremony, making their way round the house to reach the track down to the water's edge. Nicola clung on like grim death to the swaying saddle. Initially the water reached no further than the animals' knees. Only as they approached the river itself did it begin to deepen, the current sending wavelets rippling across the surface. Nicola could not have said where the track began or ended by then, but Ross seemed to know by instinct—or his horse did. There came a scary few minutes of swift-running water reaching half-way up her own legs as the riverbed was negotiated. The animals took it in their stride, never once stumbling. By the time they reached the shallows again, Nicola had begun to feel she might just make it to Santa Elena without falling off.

The flooding stretched for perhaps a quarter of a mile before slightly higher ground provided a respite. Clouds of mosquitoes made every step a torment.

The humidity was enervating. Saddle-sore already from the constant friction against her inner thighs, Nicola could only hold on and wait for an eventual end to his dreadful journey. How Ross proposed to get her to Caracas without a car she had no idea. Perhaps, after all, he would have to settle for seeing her on to a bus. That would leave her to negotiate a new passport on her own, but that couldn't be helped. He owed her nothing.

They ran into further flooded stretches along the trail, although none as extensive as the one they had left. Conversation was kept to a minimum. It took all of Ross's attention to keep them heading in the right direction. Santa Elena came into view at last, after more than an hour of hard trekking. Even smaller than Nicola had imagined from her passing glimpse of it through the small rear-window of the truck in which she had been kept prisoner, it consisted of a few narrow streets edged with tin or thatch-roofed buildings, set around a central square. The church was the most well maintained place in the immediate township, walls gleaming white in the returned sunlight. The bell tower looked the highest focal point around.

Their appearance aroused little interest among the populace, few of whom were in evidence anyway. Ross made for one building distinguishable from its neighbours only by the sign nailed to an outside wall, tying both horses to a convenient rail before coming round to help Nicola dismount.

From that height, and stiff as she was, the only way was to throw over a leg and allow herself to slide down into his arms. For a brief moment, she felt his lean muscularity at her back, the warmth of his breath on her cheek. The hands spanning her waist were firm in their grip. She wanted suddenly for him to go on holding her this way, to lean her weight against him and know the safety and security he could provide. It was Ross himself who moved abruptly away.

'Let's get to it,' he said.

Consisting of a single room, with a door at the rear that might lead to the cells, the police station was manned by an officer whose uniform had either been made for a thinner man or was a relic from the days when he himself had been of a lesser girth than his present rotundity. Dark eyes flickered from Ross to Nicola and back again every few seconds as the former explained her predicament in what sounded, to Nicola at least, very fluent Spanish. There followed a series of questions and answers, then the policeman leaned forward and rang a small bell on the battered wooden desk, barking a command at the boy who popped his head around the rear door. Ross turned back to look at Nicola.

'Seems they might have your suitcase. It was found dumped at the roadside early this morning.'

Her eyes lit up. 'And my papers, too?'

'Doubtful. Passports can be doctored to fetch a big price on the black market. Did you have any currency?'

'Barely enough to be worth stealing.'

His smile was brief. 'Depends on the viewpoint. A few bolivars will buy a loaf of bread.'

The official said something in Spanish, drawing a shake of Ross's head. Nicola wished she could understand the language, even a little. It was frustrating having her affairs discussed without being able to join in. She had been carrying her shoulder bag inside the suitcase for convenience. If her abductors had been panicked into throwing out her belongings, there was a chance that her passport and other things might prove to be intact. It would save so much trouble if they were.

The boy returned bearing a damp and dirty piece of luggage she could only just recognise as her own. It had been opened; she could see right away that the locks had been sprung. The keys had resided in the pocket of her slacks, lost during that mad flight—was it really only last night? Fatalistically, at the policeman's invitation, relayed through Ross, she went to inspect the contents, looking in dismay at the water-stained disarray of garments within. All salvageable, she supposed, with a little care and attention, but few items were instantly wearable. Her heart leapt as her probing fingers came into contact with leather. Drawing out the brown shoulderbag, she sent up a silent prayer.

The passport was gone. So was her wallet. Sinkingly, she indicated as much to the Venezuelan. To her surprise, he opened a drawer to take out the missing items, carefully comparing the photograph inside the passport with its owner, as if still in some faint doubt as to the validity of her claim. A pen was proffered, and she was asked to sign for the return of her belongings. After that, it seemed they were free to go.

Outside again, Nicola screwed up her eyes against the strong sunlight as she looked at Ross.

'Is that all?'

He shrugged. 'I told you there was probably nothing much they could do. Those two will be miles away by now. Be grateful you got your stuff back. Whoever picked it up must have an honest streak'.

'I *am* grateful,' she said. 'I can't tell you what a relief it is.' She hesitated before tagging on, 'So what next?'

Grey eyes remained veiled. 'Seems like it's back to the ranch for the present. We're cut off.'

'For how long?'

'As long as it takes to clear the roads. Maybe a day, maybe two. Providing we don't get any more rain, it shouldn't be longer than that.'

'I could stay here in Santa Elena,' she ventured, and saw his lips thin.

'No, you couldn't. We'll grab a couple of *tortillas*, then head for home while the going's good.'

'I'm sorry.' She scarcely knew what else to say. 'I realise you'd rather be on your own.'

'I'll survive.' He wasn't giving an inch. 'Your bag's going to be something of a problem. I'll need more rope.'

'You could use the leading rein,' Nicola suggested, trying to make amends. 'I'll be OK going back.'

'Sure you will.' He turned away. 'There's only one place to eat. Just don't expect too much.'

She had given up anticipating anything, thought Nicola wryly. From now on, she took everything as it came.

The bar was on a back street, dark and dingy and obviously not much frequented by the women of the town. That Ross himself was no stranger there was made evident when the barman greeted him by name. That and '*tortillas*' were the only words Nicola understood in the resulting conversation, although, judging from the speculative glances cast her way, she was the main topic under discussion.

The food turned out to be not only edible but extremely enjoyable—if one turned a blind eye to the somewhat suspect cutlery. The accompanying coffee was pre-sugared to a sweetness Nicola found cloying, but she drank it regardless and felt surprisingly better for it.

Ross was the one off his food this time. After a couple of bites he pushed the plate away, contenting himself with a glass of what she assumed to be whisky. He seemed abstracted, his thoughts far away from this place, this time. His whole attitude was detached, as if he had given up living and settled for just existing.

'At least there isn't going to be any need for you to come right through to Caracas with me,' she ventured at length, unable to bear the lack of communication. 'All I'm going to need is a loan from the Consulate to get me home.'

He studied her for a moment before replying. 'You think it's going to be that simple?'

'Why not? Others have done it. After all, I'm a British citizen.'

'Who has to reach the people she needs to reach first.'

Blue eyes darkened. 'You're saying I might not make it on my own?'

'It happened once, it can happen again. I'm not saying it will, but the chance is there. I'm not likely to rest easy till you're safely tucked away on a flight home. If you want to pay anybody back, you can pay me.'

She drew in a breath. 'I can't accept money from you!'

His smile was faint. 'You were willing enough to accept it from the Consulate.'

'That's different.'

'Sure is. It will take longer, for one thing. Still, suit yourself.'

Biting her lip, she said wryly, 'I shouldn't look a gift horse in the mouth, should I? Thanks, Ross. I really do appreciate the offer.'

'It's only money.'

'And your time.'

'I'm hardly pushed for that, either.' He drained the glass and put it down with a decisive little thud. 'We'd better get on back before it starts again.'

Nicola glanced towards the window where the sunlight was making valiant efforts to break through the grime. 'There doesn't seem much chance of that.'

'Not right this minute, maybe. I've learned not to

take anything for granted.' He was standing as he spoke, reaching for the suitcase he had lodged under the table while they ate. 'I still have to stow this.'

She trailed after him reluctantly. Returning to the house was the only possible course to take, but that didn't make it any easier to accept. Ross resented her presence, that much was obvious. He probably regretted ever having got himself involved. Not that he'd had much choice in the matter, considering the circumstances. It would have taken a hard heart indeed to abandon her to her fate.

There was little appreciable drop in water levels on the way back, but the sun kept on shining. The heat was oppressive.

'How have you stood this climate all these months?' she asked at one point, when they were able to ride abreast on dry land for a while. 'It has to be different from California.'

His laugh had an edge. 'That has to be the understatement of the year! The rains haven't worried me any. I haven't been going out in it all that much.'

Nicola slanted a glance, taking in the hardness of thigh muscle beneath the tight-fitting jeans, the easy familiarity of his hands on the rein. 'You haven't exactly been letting yourself run to seed, either,' she commented. 'Do you work on the farm?'

'Not noticeably. Hardly my style. There are other ways of staying in good physical shape. Riding, for instance.'

She said ruefully, 'The only thing it seems to be doing for me is making every muscle feel as if it's been kicked!'

'Only because you're using ones you've never used before. They'll feel worse tomorrow.'

'Thanks!'

This time, the laugh held amusement. 'You'll get over it. The next time we make this journey it will be by car.'

'I'll cling to that thought.' She waited a moment before adding doggedly, 'So how *do* you pass the time?'

Ross didn't answer right away. She had almost accepted that he wasn't going to answer at all, when he said, 'I've been working on a film script.'

'Oh?' She scarcely knew what comment to make. 'I didn't realise you wrote as well.'

His lips twisted. 'As well as what?'

'Directed.' She kept her tone level. 'That isn't usual, it is?'

'It isn't unknown to have the same person write, direct *and* take the lead in a film,' he returned. 'But for me, no, it isn't usual. Call it a therapy.'

'You mean it's autobiographical?'

He gave her a swift glance, eyes suddenly narrowed. 'What makes you say that?'

Her shrug was overcasual. 'I took a basic psychology course in school. Writing down one's thoughts and feelings helps clear the mind.'

'Is that right?' There was cynicism in the line of his mouth. 'Maybe you'd better stick to acting. An amateur shrink I don't need!'

'I wasn't offering an analysis,' she retorted. 'You asked me a question, I gave you an answer. End of session.'

'You're too smart for your own good,' he advised on a curt note.

'For yours, perhaps.' She wasn't about to be put down. 'The trouble with men like you is you see all women as mentally inferior—no matter what their age!'

Up to that point she had experienced little trouble with her mount. The sudden whinny and rearing motion caught her totally off balance. One minute she was sitting in her saddle, the next she was lying in the dirt with all the breath knocked out of her and the sound of galloping hooves drumming in her ears. She had a brief and terrifying glimpse of something long and sinuous disappearing into the undergrowth edging the trail, then Ross was at her side, concern in the grey eyes.

'Don't move for a minute. You took a bad tumble.' He ran his hands quickly over her limbs, watching her face for any sign of pain. 'OK?'

'I think so.' Nicola was only just beginning to sort out her jumbled thoughts. 'What happened?'

'Basking snake,' he said. 'Your horse scented it before I saw it. Can you stand up?'

She accepted the helping hand he held out, rising gingerly to her feet. Just bruising, she reckoned, although she was probably going to be stiff and sore later on. The arm he was using to support her weight for the moment felt good. She would like to keep it there. When he let go of her, she only just stopped herself from clutching at him. Fear, of course, she told herself. He represented a measure of safety—from snakes, at least.

'My fault,' he acknowledged. 'I should have been watching the road more closely.'

'How do we catch him?' she asked.

'We don't try. He'll be OK. The cats don't hunt by day.'

Her eyes lifted sharply to his face. 'Cats?'

'There are a couple of pumas in the area, at least. Don't worry about it. They rarely attack humans.' He went to secure his own horse, which was standing quietly by the roadside. 'You're going to have to ride with me. Think you can make it back to the house?'

'If it's a choice between that and staying here, with God knows what around, I'll make it,' she said unsteadily. 'I must have been mad even thinking about spending a year in a place like this!'

'You obviously didn't do too much homework,' Ross agreed. 'It's no country for the faint-hearted. There are seven species of cat alone, to say nothing of the snakes and crocodiles. Caracas might be only a hundred miles or so away, but it's light years in time. If you want a job in Venezuela, that's the place to be.' He was watching her as he spoke, assessing her state of health. 'You'll be OK. Your colour's coming back.'

Which was more than could be said for her nerve, thought Nicola wryly as he swung himself up into the saddle. With the suitcase fastened on behind, there was only one place for her. Leaning down, Ross proffered a hand. 'Stick your foot in the stirrup and I'll do the rest.'

Obeying with some difficulty, owing to the distance of the stirrup from the ground to start with, she found herself lifted and hauled into position across his thighs, held securely in place by the arms stretched either side of her to the reins. Her head was on a level with his shoulder, her eyes within inches of his jawline. This close, she could see the shadow under the skin that would become tomorrow's beard, catch the male scent of him. His mouth was firm and well cut, his chin just slightly cleft. She knew a swiftly suppressed desire to touch a finger to it. Whatever else this man might be, he was no murderer. Her instincts couldn't be that far out.

'Relax,' he said as he put the animals into motion. 'I won't let you fall.'

She was half-way there already, Nicola reflected wryly, if only on a physical level. She wanted to penetrate those defences of his, to find the man he really was. If there was danger in that at all, it was only to her own inner emotions.

They reached the house without further mishap, to find the runaway there before them and Ramón about to set out in search of the missing element. He accepted Nicola's return with indifference.

Maria was more voluble, haranguing Ross in no uncertain tone.

'She warned me earlier that we'd be unlikely to get through for a couple of days,' he admitted when the housekeeper had gone. 'Like most women, she couldn't forgo saying I told you so!'

'Well, she did,' Nicola returned mildly. 'And, like most men, you choose to ignore the advice. I appreciate why, of course.'

'Do you?' He gave her an oblique glance. 'You'd better go and sort your stuff out. See what can be salvaged.'

Maria had taken the suitcase with her. Nicola found her already in the process of unpacking the contents, giving vent to muttered exclamations at the state of the garments. Everything, Nicola gathered, would have to be washed before becoming wearable again. That left her with the shirt and slacks she had taken with her this morning by way of a change from her present soiled outfit.

Ross was not in evidence when she eventually made her way back to the living-room. A faint tapping sound drew her to a window overlooking the side of the house, where some attempt had been made to cultivate a bit of a garden. The tapping sound emanated from a small, thatch-roofed hut set some distance away from the main building. Nicola identified it as coming from a typewriter. Therapeutic or not, Ross appeared to be in full flow. She would have dearly loved to know just what he *was* writing.

There were books aplenty on floor-to-ceiling shelves in one of the chimney-breast alcoves, some of them in English. Nicola selected a paperback copy of a James A Michener epic and settled down on one of the overstuffed sofas to read, but her mind refused to make sense of the words. Eventually, she gave it up and allowed her thoughts to range back over the past days, reliving the horror of it all. If Ross hadn't come along when he did, they would have caught up with her for sure. Either that or she might have fallen prey to one of those seven species of big cat he had spoken of. How did he stand it day after day in these surroundings? Even when the sun shone, it was no paradise.

He was still typing, almost non-stop. Ideas must be coming thick and fast. For a moment, she wondered if perhaps he might even be using the last twenty-four hours' events as background material, then dismissed the thought as unlikely. Her head throbbed dully. She thought of trying to ask Maria if there was any aspirin in the house, but it all seemed too much trouble. The headache would go off if she stayed here quietly and just rested her eyes . . .

Ross was sitting on the edge of the sofa at her side when she awoke. He was holding her wrist, a finger on her pulse, that same look of concern on his face.

'I thought you'd passed out,' he said. 'You were slumped across the arm like a sack of potatoes. How do you feel?'

Terrible, she wanted to say. Her skin was burning hot, her throat so dry it rasped when she swallowed. 'Not too good,' she murmered weakly. 'I think I might have caught a chill, or something.'

'Let's hope that's all you've caught,' he said on a grim note. 'Anyway, you'll be better in bed.'

Nicola made a small sound of protest as he got up and hoisted her in his arms. 'I can walk!'

'Maybe, but this is quicker. You've got a fever.'

She didn't need him to tell her that, she thought peevishly, feeling too ill to protest any more. It had come on so suddenly. Apart from the headache, she had felt all right when she had gone to sleep.

Reaching the bedroom, Ross set her down carefully on the bed, taking another narrowed look at her before striding back to the door to call for Maria. The woman came at once, drying her hands on her calico apron. A few words from Ross were all that was necessary to put her in the picture. After that, she took charge, showing the former out of the room and closing the door before coming back to help Nicola out of her clothing and between clean sheets. No nightdress this time. It was probably in the wash, along with her own things.

Ross came back, carrying a glass of some clear liquid that looked like water and smelled horrible.

'Quinine,' he supplied. 'Apart from aspirin, it's about the only medication available. You'll manage it better if you can sit up a bit.'

The sheet slipped down as she did so, but she was beyond caring overmuch. A wave of nausea almost overcame her. It was with relief that she lay back on the pillow again. Ross stood looking down at her, chewing on his lower lip as if contemplating what course of action to take next.

'The nearest medic of any use to us is in Velida,' he said at length. 'I could send Ramón to fetch him, but it's going to take some hours.'

'I'll be all right,' Nicola assured him, putting on a false front. 'It's just a chill.'

'Let's hope you're right.' His hand rested fleetingly against her forehead. 'Try and get some more sleep.'

CHAPTER THREE

NICOLA did sleep, although it was fitfully, her mind troubled by nightmares she couldn't remember on waking. Her whole body was soaked in perspiration, her head pounding fit to burst. The door must have been open and Ross hovering somewhere close, because he appeared almost at once in answer to her croaked plea for water, lips tautening when he saw her. Water was brought, but she was allowed only sips. The room swam about her when she attempted to lift her head.

Time dissolved into a series of fleeting impressions after that: disembodied faces floating above her, voices echoing from some far distance. She was lying in a cool stream, the water trickling deliciously over her breasts and thighs, then suddenly the coolness was gone and fire was sweeping through her, burning her up, making her cry out. She was trapped in some dark place, unable to break free, her mind struggling against the horror that threatened to overwhelm it.

And then at last, at long, long last, a total and blessed oblivion.

It was dark in the room when she finally awoke. She felt physically weak, but her mind was clear again. Sitting up cautiously, she switched on the bedside lamp, conscious of the distant throbbing of the generator as she looked at her watch. Nine-thirty. Almost five hours since Ross had put her to bed. Whatever it was she had been suffering from, it had run its course in a relatively short time. She even felt ready for food.

The door of the wardrobe across the room stood partly ajar, revealing a full row of hanging garments. Maria must have been in while she slept and brought back her things, she realised. In this climate, nothing would take all that long to dry, of course. All the same, the woman must have worked like fury to get everything back into spick-and-span shape so quickly. She must remember to thank her when she saw her again. That was one Spanish word she could use with confidence.

Ross came into the room without knocking. Only then, as she met the grey eyes, did she suddenly recall her lack of nightwear earlier. The cotton pyjamas she was wearing now were her own, bought for practicality rather than aesthetic appeal. Maria must have put her into them.

'How are you feeling?' he asked. 'Fancy some food?'

'I wouldn't mind.' She attempted a laugh, surprised by the tinny little sound. 'I feel as if I hadn't eaten for days!'

'The day before yesterday, to be exact,' he said. 'You've been through a bad time.'

Two days! She could scarcely believe it. Yet he certainly had no reason to lie to her. 'What was it?' she asked.

'Not what I was afraid of, or you wouldn't be over it so quickly.' Ross shrugged. 'Could be any of a dozen different bugs bit you. We broke the fever this morning. You've slept like a log since then.'

Nicola looked at him from under concealing lashes. 'We?'

'I helped Maria from time to time sponging you down.' He said it levelly. 'Don't concern yourself. You don't have anything I haven't seen before.'

'I'm sure.' She tried to look at it rationally.

'Er . . . thanks, anyway.'

His lips twitched. 'No hassle. I'm just thankful you're OK. We couldn't get hold of the medic. He was visiting some patient up country. I'll see about some food.'

Left alone again, Nicola attempted to get out of the bed, only to sink back into the pillows with a murmur of frustration at the lack of strength in her limbs. It would soon pass, she told herself. She was young and healthy. This was no more than a temporary set-back. By tomorrow . . .

By tomorrow, she needed to have some plan worked out. Ross had been landed with her long enough. After two days, the water should have receded far enough to allow her passage through to Caracas. His offer to fund her journey home to England still had to be thought about. It was going to be a long time before she was in any position to pay him back. He was virtually a stranger, after all. How could she borrow such a sum from a man she was never even likely to see again?

That latter thought alone brought despondency in its wake.

She was sitting propped up on the pillows when Ross returned with a steaming bowl of thick vegetable soup.

'There's chicken in it, too,' he said, depositing the tray across her knees. 'Can you cope like that?'

'I think so.' Nicola eyed him a little uncomfortably as he took the chair nearby. 'You don't need to stay.'

'I thought you might like the company,' he returned on an easy note. 'Tell me if you'd rather be on your own.'

'No.' The denial came out a little too quickly; she made some attempt to temper the impression she might have given. 'You can tell me what the weather's been doing the last two days. Are we still cut off?'

'Not to any great extent. I got the car through to Santa Elena this afternoon without too much trouble. The main roads are clear anyway, so we can leave as soon as you're fit to travel.'

Nicola concentrated on the spoon she was raising to her lips. Wasn't that exactly what she had been thinking herself not five minutes ago! Yes, came the answer, but there was a great deal of difference between thinking and doing. Back home lay the same hand-to-mouth existence—the same struggle for recognition. She wasn't ready to face it again. Not yet.

'Have you heard from Carlos yet?' she asked, not from any great need to know, but because it was something else to say.

'No,' he admitted.

'You're not worried about him?'

'Not unduly. He'll be back when he's finished what he has to do.'

'So you know where he's gone?'

'Caracas. He makes the trip once a year to keep his affairs in order.'

Her glance encompassed the simple furnishings, the bare white walls. 'I shouldn't have imagined him a man of very great means.'

Ross said evenly, 'Never judge a man by his surroundings. Carlos lives this way by choice. Escaping the twentieth century, you might call it.'

'Life isn't that grim,' she defended, and saw the firm mouth pull into a faint smile.

'You haven't lived it long enough to make unqualified statements.'

'I've lived long enough,' she retaliated, 'to know that you can't just turn your back on it because things haven't worked out the way they might have.'

The lean features tautened a fraction. 'If it's advice we're dishing out, you'd be better off concerning yourself with your own future. What are you planning on doing when you get back home?'

'I don't know,' Nicola admitted. 'Without a job,
I'm going to have to rely on the State for somewhere
to live. That means a hostel, I imagine.'

'Sounds grim.' The pause was brief. 'If it's just a
case of money . . .'

She shook her head, hair falling forward over her
face. 'You're doing enough. I can't accept any more.'

'Pride's an indulgence at times,' he stated. 'One you
can't afford right now. How good an actress are you?'

Blue eyes came up to meet grey, lit by sudden
resolution. 'Good enough not to give up without a
fight. I'll find a part if it kills me!'

'Rather defeat the purpose, wouldn't it?'

Her smile was reluctant. 'I'm better at speaking the
words than writing them.' She took a final mouthful
of the soup, then put the spoon down. 'I'm sorry, I
can't finish this.'

'You've done pretty well.' Ross got to his feet to
come and lift the tray from her lap, looking down at
her with an unreadable expression. 'Try and get
some more sleep. Tomorrow we'll start sorting
something out.'

'It isn't your problem,' she said, sinking down
obediently into the pillows again.

'True, but I'm better equipped than you are to
handle it.' He was already turning away to the door.
'I'll be in earshot if you want anything.'

Like comfort? she thought in sudden aching need.
She felt so mixed up, so unsure of herself. She would
find a part if it killed her, she had told him. A brave
statement indeed when it was doubt in her ability as
an actress that had driven her into applying for the
job in Venezuela in the first place. There was so much
competition, so much talent out there—and so much
hardship. To face it at all, one needed total
commitment to the belief that success lay just around
the corner. She wasn't even sure of her own mind any

more—not where the acting profession was concerned, at any rate. There had to be easier ways of making a living.

She slept again, waking some time after midnight to a house which was silent and still. What noise there was came from the insect life outside, with the occasional cry of some animal from afar. Listening, Nicola wondered if it could be one of the pumas Ross had spoken of, although it seemed unlikely that a hunting animal would make any sound at all.

The weakness was still there when she sat upright, if not as pronounced as before. It took her a moment or two to struggle into her light cotton wrap. The bathroom was down the end of the corridor, almost opposite the room she knew Ross occupied. Only on emerging again did she note that the door to the latter stood ajar. The generator had been switched off long since, making moonlight the only source. One glance into the room was enough to reveal it empty, the bedclothes tumbled, as if shoved back by an impatient hand. Nicolas hesitated only a moment before giving way to the urge within her, not even sure what her intention really was.

She found him sitting out on the veranda, apparently oblivious to the relative coolness of the night air. He was wearing a calf-length white towelling robe and little else from what she could see, his feet pushed into raffia sandles.

'You shouldn't be out here,' he said as she paused in the doorway. 'Get a chill on top of what you've just been through, and you'll finish up in hospital rather than on a plane home.'

'I'm not cold,' she denied. 'I saw your room was empty and wondered if you were working on your script again.'

The excuse sounded lame, even to her own ears. That

Ross heard it the same way was evident from the sudden slant of his lip. 'If I had been, I'd hardly be in the mood for company.'

Nicola was glad of the concealing darkness. 'Obviously, I shouldn't have intruded on you in that case. I needed to stretch my legs for a minute or two, that's all.'

He was silent for a moment or two, studying her. When he did speak, it was with the same flat intonation. 'It's finished.'

Her response was instinctive. 'So you don't have any further excuse to stay on here?'

His mouth straightened. 'You take a lot of chances.'

'I don't think so. As you told me the other morning, even if you had killed your wife, it wouldn't mean you had homicidal tendencies towards every woman.' The pause was timed. 'I don't believe it, anyway.'

Grey eyes held blue for a long, tense moment, taking on some new expression. He said softly, 'I really think you mean that.'

'I do.' She was anxious to convince him. 'You're not the type to commit murder.'

The laugh was short. 'Back to psychological profiles again, are we? There is no *type* when it comes to crimes of passion, honey! We're all of us capable of the worst. God knows, I wanted to kill her. She . . .' He broke off abruptly, shaking his head. 'Forget it. It's all water under the bridge.'

Something in her couldn't let go. Not now, when she had come so close. 'It might help to talk about it.'

'To you?' The derision was meant to hurt. 'What good could a kid like you do me?'

'I could listen,' said Nicola, refusing to take offence. 'I bet you never discussed it with anyone.'

'Apart from the law, you mean? I spent thirty-six hours in custody. Believe me, they examined every angle. If it hadn't been proved that the brake cable hadn't been tampered with, I might be there yet, awaiting trial.'

'That has to take some forgetting,' Nicola agreed. 'But it's over now. Time to get back to work. Are you planning on using that screenplay?'

Something flickered in the grey eyes. 'There's such a thing as backing.'

'I know that. But you could get it—if the script is any good, that it.'

'Thinking of offering an opinion, by any chance?'

'No.' She kept her tone level. 'There's a world of difference between film and theatre.'

'You're hardly qualified in either sphere.' He moved abruptly. 'Let's drop it.'

This time, the rebuff was too pointed to ignore. 'Sorry I disturbed you.'

She was turning back to the door when he said, low-toned, 'So what's new?'

Her heart beating suddenly faster, she glanced back at him. 'I don't think I . . .'

'You understand OK. You're no dumb blonde. You've been disturbing me since you got here. If you were five years older, I'd know what to do about it.'

'If I were five years older, I probably wouldn't be in this situation to start with,' Nicola responded, abandoning her stance. She added softly, 'I didn't realise you felt the same way.'

'You still don't.'

'Meaning it's so different?' Her head was up, her eyes challenging. 'How would you know?'

He smiled at little. 'I'm a good guesser.'

'But a lousy judge.' She was letting instinct do the talking. 'I told you before, I'm no child. I'm as capable of being attracted to a man as the next.'

He studied her for a long moment, his expression

difficult to define with any accuracy. 'OK,' he said at
length, 'so which room do we use?'

'Neither.' She refused to rise to the taunt. 'I'm not
one of your Hollywood bimboes, ready to jump into
bed at the drop of a hat.' A flush stained her cheeks as
she realised what she had said. 'Oh, lord, I'm sorry! I
didn't mean it to sound as it . . .'

'As if you were referring to my wife?' he finished for
her as her voice petered away. 'It's only the truth.'

'But not always?' she ventured.

'No.' There was a pause. When he spoke again, it
was on a rougher note. 'You come from a different
world. Arlene was very little older than you are now
when I first met her, but you're poles apart.'

'She was very beautiful,' Nicola murmured.

'She was more than that. Beauty on its own can be
boring, especially in places like LA, where it's
commonplace. Arlene had that extra something that set
her out from the rest. Not that she knew how to use it.'

'Until you taught her.'

'Yes.' He was hooked now, the identity of his listener
probably forgotten as he looked back into the past. 'She
was my creation, in a sense. I taught her how to walk,
how to speak, how to dress, how to project. She had
enough acting ability to really make impact in certain
chosen roles, only the studio had other ideas. They
wanted to use her as another sex queen—a modern-day
Jane Russell.'

'But you still agreed to direct her?'

'If I did it was in the hope of salvaging something of
the career I had planned for her.' He added flatly, 'I
failed.'

'The public didn't seem to think so.'

'The public!' he snapped, on a derisive notes.
'Brainwashing, that's all. Selling refrigerators to
Eskimoes is child's play to publicity guys.'

Nicola was leaning against the back of one of the chairs, not wanting to interrupt the mood by moving to sit down. 'How did she feel about it herself?'

'She revelled in it. Trouble was, she started playing the same role off-screen as well as on it.'

She said tentatively, 'Perhaps if you'd loved her it might have been different.'

The dark head jerked. 'What makes you so sure I didn't?'

'The way you just talked about her. If you'd loved her, she would have been right for you the way she was, not the way you wanted her to be.'

It was a moment before he responded. 'Did it occur to you that she might have known what she was doing, too? I said she didn't know how to use what she had, I didn't say she wasn't aware of having it.' He got abruptly to his feet. 'There's no point in talking about it now. I'm going in. If you've any sense, you'll do the same.'

'Ross.' She hadn't meant to say it; the words were drawn from her by some instinct beyond her control. 'Don't make me leave tomorrow.'

He paused to look at her. 'Who said anything about tomorrow? The day after, maybe.'

She returned his gaze with what equanimity she could muster. 'I'm asking you to let me stay for a while.'

His lips twisted. 'I'm a visitor here, too.'

'Until Carlos gets back, then.' She was trying her best not to plead. 'A breathing space, that's all I'm asking.'

His eyes dropped to scan her slender figure, coming back to the cloud of pale hair, the pure, fine features, and a muscle contracted alongside his mouth. 'I'm not cut out to play the avuncular role,' he said. 'You're a very lovely girl, and I've been a long time without a woman. I might lose my head.'

'I don't think so.' Her tone was soft. 'Anyway, it takes two, and I've no intention of losing mine.'

Ross's smile was not without humour. 'You take too much on trust.' He paused, studying her, the hard lines of his face subtly softened. 'What difference is a few days, or even weeks, going to make? You have to go back some time.'

'I know that.' Nicola lifted her shoulders. 'It's just as I said, a breathing space. When the time comes, I'll take you up on that offer to finance my return home.'

'If you do stay,' he said after a moment, 'I think we should make some attempt to contact these people you were supposed to be joining.'

She gave him a straight look. 'You think I was lying about them?'

'Why on earth should I do that?' He sounded genuinely surprised. 'Don't you want to know what happened?'

'Yes, of course.' It was impossible to admit that she no longer cared. At best, the job would have been a stop-gap, at worst, a prison. To be here in the Venezuelan jungle for a few days at her own choice was a different matter altogether from being forced to stick it out for a year.

'We'll go tomorrow, if you feel up to it,' he said. 'Better get back to bed, before you finish up with a chill.'

There was no point, she acknowledged, in further discussion. He had said all he was going to say for now. But the spark of warmth in the grey eyes had not been imaginary. That in itself was a breakthrough.

The river was back to normal flow after the flood, scarcely covering the lower part of the tyre treads where they forded the stretch. The sun's heat was palpable, the humidity overwhelming. Despite the open window,

Nicola could feel perspiration springing from every pore. Ross exhibited no obvious discomfort, although the white T-shirt he was wearing had a damp patch across the back, she noted, when he eased himself away from the seat for a moment.

This enquiry they were to make aroused mixed feelings. Supposing the family had turned up again when they reached the plantation? Supposing, even, that the man she had paid to transport her from the town had taken her to the wrong place? She had been unable to find anyone who could speak English, and her few words of Spanish could so easily have been misunderstood. Unlikely, perhaps, but if the job should still prove to be available what should she do? More to the point, what would Ross expect her to do? His attitude towards her might have altered a little, but she could hardly take advantage of his financial help under those circumstances.

She was crossing her bridges before she came to them, she told herself at that point. There would be time enough to start worrying if and when it was proved necessary.

In the cramped and squalid confines of the truck in which she had been imprisoned, the journey that evening had seemed to take an age. In reality, it turned out to be a little more than half an hour from Santa Elena to Velida. The latter was a considerably larger township, with a thriving population. Driving through the thronged and narrow streets, Nicola recalled her mounting desperation as she tried to find someone who could understand and appreciate her predicament. It had been sheer relief that had blinded her to the possible purpose behind Rodrigo's and Juan's approach, she realised that now.

Ross stopped to ask directions out to the Cordova plantation. At least she had got that much right, thought Nicola, viewing the white-walled house when they drove on to the property. The last time she had been here the windows had been shuttered, the doors locked. Seeing the man who came out onto the veranda as they drew up, her heart sank like a stone.

'If you're looking for Velida, it's about five kilometres,' he said pleasantly, addressing Ross, who was nearest. 'Come far, have you?'

'Some,' Ross acknowledged. 'Is your name Crossman?'

'No, I'm his replacement. Only got in a couple of days ago.' The other man paused. 'Why did you want him?'

'It's for me, really,' Nicola put in. 'I was supposed to start a job here last week, looking after their little boy.'

He shook his head. 'I wouldn't know about that. The only story I've got is that Mrs Crossman took off with the boy and he went after them. Left a load of stuff here, so he might be back. Afraid I can't tell you anything else.'

'Thanks, anyway.' Nicola was hard put to it to sound properly rueful. 'Sorry to have troubled you.'

'No trouble. Only sorry I can't be of more help. You could try the company offices in Caracas. They might have more information.'

'Right,' she said. 'And thanks again.'

'Sounds like something blew up in their faces,' commented Ross when they were on their way again. 'Maybe you're as well out of it.'

Nicola was sure of it. 'So what now?' she asked.

'Same as before, I guess.' He was watching the road ahead. 'Back to the house for starters.'

'*Rancho*,' she corrected, trying for a light note.

'*Rancho*, then. The glance he gave her was tolerant. 'You're more adaptable than most.'

'I've had practice,' she said.

'Maybe as well, considering.' There was a pause, a change of tone. 'What do you plan to on doing when you get back home?'

'I don't know,' she confessed. 'Look for a job, I suppose.'

'In the theatre?'

'If possible.' Her smile was wry. 'It's difficult gaining experience without the experience, if you know what I mean.'

'Catch twenty-two.' He was silent for a moment before adding, 'I've contacts in British television. Maybe I . . .'

'Thanks, but no thanks. If I make it at all, it has to be because I have talent, not because I happen to know the right people.'

Broad shoulders lifted in a shrug. 'Laudable, but not likely to take you far. Get the part first, then prove how good you are. For every role going, there are a few hundred hopefuls out there vying for it. You use whatever pull you've got, if you've any sense.'

'I can't help the way I feel,' she stated stubbornly. 'Even if that does make me a fool.'

'I didn't say you were a fool. Fool*ish* at times, maybe.' He cast another glance, the smile lacking in mockery. 'Are you really twenty-one?'

'My birthdate is on my passport,' said Nicola, registering the sudden quickening of her pulses. 'If I appear younger to you, it's probably because I've led a sheltered life up to now.'

'Unlike the twenty-one-year-olds I've been used to,' finished Ross on a dry note. 'Fair comment.'

'There must be some normal, well adjusted people, even in your part of the world,' she protested, and drew another smile.

'Sure there are. I even know a few myself.'

'You actually live in Hollywood?' she ventured.

'Not by choice.'

Arlene's, of course, thought Nicola. He must have cared enough to indulge her in that sphere, at least.

'I suppose you closed the place up when you came away.' she said.

He shook his head. 'There's a married couple who take care of it.'

'Can you trust them?'

The shrug came again. 'It's a bit late now to start thinking about it.'

She gave him an oblique glance. 'You have to go back some time, too.'

'Maybe.' He added on a more brusque note, 'You ask a lot of questions.'

'It's the only way to get answers.' She put out an impulsive hand to touch his arm, feeling the muscle contract beneath her fingers. 'It isn't just idle curiosity, Ross.'

He pulled in suddenly at the side of the road, his hands white-knuckled on the wheel. 'I was doing OK until you dropped in,' he said with sudden savagery.

'You mean, you'd driven it under.' Her voice was soft, soothing, her every instinct reaching out to him. 'You didn't kill her. You can't spend the rest of your life shutting yourself away because some people who don't know you very well think you might have.'

He turned his head to look at her, searching her face with an expression so intent, it seared her brain. 'You don't know me at all. What makes you so sure I was telling you the truth?'

'I suppose you'd have to call it a gut feeling,' she said.

There was feeling now as she looked back into the grey eyes, a stirring of emotion that started way down deep. The mask had been stripped away, the vulnerability exposed. She said his name softly, not even sure what it was she wanted until she saw the flame spring alive.

His kiss shattered every defence she had in its blind, seeking passion. She moved closer to him, arms curving about his shoulders, fingers winding into his thick, dark hair. It felt so good in his arms, so utterly and completely right. She wanted to stay there for ever, not thinking, just being.

It was Ross himself who broke it off, but he didn't let her go, his face buried in the fall of her hair.

'You should have let me take you back to Caracas,' he said thickly. 'Have you any idea what I've been going through these last few days?'

'No,' she whispered. 'But that's only because you wouldn't let me in.'

'I dared not.' His tone was rueful. 'I thought I'd got it licked until just now. I was kidding myself.' He put her away from him with an abrupt movement, straightening in his seat. 'You're leaving,' he declared, reaching for the ignition. 'We can make Caracas before nightfall.'

'I don't want to go.' If it had been true before, it was doubly so now, Nicola thought blindly. She had glimpsed a different Ross, a man she wanted desperately to find again. She couldn't do that in Caracas. 'I *won't* go,' she added. 'Not unless you can tell me with honesty that you don't want me here.'

His gaze lingered on the fullness of her mouth, taking on a look of resignation. 'I can't do that.'

'Then I'm staying.' She added huskily, 'Not just for your sake, for mine, too. I don't have anything to go back for.'

One lean brown hand came out as if of its own volition to gently smooth her cheek, the touch alone sending tremors along her spine. 'What about your career?'

'I don't have a career. I'm not even sure I want a career—not in theatre, at any rate. What ambition I had seems to have vanished.'

'That isn't the impression you gave yesterday.'

'I was trying to convince myself as much as you.'

The hand had moved round beneath the fall of hair to the nape of her neck, his thumb lightly caressing. 'So, what other plans do you have for the future?'

'I don't know,' confessed Nicola. Her senses were swimming, her whole inner body concentrated on his touch. The grey eyes had lost all their coldness, their aloofness. 'I hadn't thought that far ahead.'

'You can't stay here for ever.'

'Neither can you.' Her own hand lifted to trace the shape of his mouth with a forefinger, feeling his reaction with a sensual thrill. 'It's decision time for both of us, isn't it?'

'You're not making it easy.' Ross caught the hand, turning it over to press it to his lips. 'When I came out here, I was as far down as I could get—and most of it my own fault. You were right, I didn't love Arlene. Not enough, anyway. It was my pride she hurt most. I didn't kill her, but I wanted to. Enough to give me one hell of a guilt complex when she went over that cliff. I couldn't face the publicity, the sense of being still under suspicion even after I was released. I'm not sure I'm ready to do it even now.'

'It would be a nine-day wonder if you went back,' she said. 'Probably not even that. You have a talent most people would give their eye-teeth for. You can't let it go to waste!'

He said softly, 'You could try taking your own advice.'

'Except that my talent hasn't been proven.'

'For acting, maybe not. For everything else . . .' He drew her forwards and kissed her again, cherishing her mouth. 'You're like nobody I ever met before,' he murmured against her lips. 'I want to make love to you, Nicola.'

'I rather thought,' she whispered, 'that's what you were doing.'

'You may be young,' he said, 'but you're not that naïve.'

'I'm not that young, either,' she denied. 'What do years matter?'

'Right now, not a lot.' He was smiling, the austerity gone from his features. 'Live for today, is that what you're saying?'

'I don't know what I'm saying,' she confessed. 'I only know I want to be with you, Ross.'

Just for a moment, there was cynicism in his eyes. 'All because I happened to be around at the right time?'

'I suppose that had some bearing, initially,' she acknowledged, trying to be honest about it. 'I had to put trust in someone. You seemed a good enough candidate.'

'Even after you realised who I was?'

'Even then. If you'd been calculating enough to plan that accident, you wouldn't have been here in the first place. People who do things like that don't normally feel anything outside of the fear of getting found out, and you'd already been cleared.' Her voice tremored a little. 'If you hadn't come along that night . . .'

'Don't think about it. It didn't happen.' He held her close for a moment, releasing her with reluctance. 'We'd better get back to the house.'

They neither of them said very much on the way. Nicola felt oddly detached from reality, as if all this was part of a dream. From time to time, she stole a glance at the lean profile, wondering what Ross was thinking. He had opened up to her back there—bared his very soul. Did he regret it now?

And what of herself? Did what she felt for this man stem from within, or had she simply been carried along on the crest of his own need? Was what she felt for him love, or merely empathy? Physically, she wanted what he wanted, but not on its own.

It wasn't until they had drawn up at the house and the ignition had been switched off that Ross made any reference to what had passed between them.

'If you want to change your mind,' he said, 'there's still time to make Caracas.'

She looked at him then, for a moment seeing only the old Ross, cold and shuttered, then her vision cleared, her emotions crystallising. 'I haven't changed my mind,' she said. 'I'm staying.'

The flash of relief in his eyes was all the confirmation she needed. Whatever came of this relationship of theirs, it was a mutual understanding they were sharing right now.

CHAPTER FOUR

NICOLA had never been as happy as during the following few days. The outside world had become a distant country, Ross himself a different person. At some point, they were going to make love, and they both knew it, but he made no attempt to hurry the moment.

Under his instruction, and with a careful damping down of her natural caution, she learned to ride a horse, although, as he himself said, these were not the ideal animals on which to learn.

'I never found much time for it back home,' he admitted on one occasion when they were returning from a late afternoon ride. 'Too busy working.'

It was the first time he had made any casual reference to the life he had left behind all those months before. Nicola kept the question casual, too.

'Don't you miss it?'

'The job maybe. The people?' He shrugged. 'Some more than others.'

'I expect,' she said, 'you know all the big stars.'

Ross laughed. 'I'm acquainted with a few. I was never really part of the Hollywood set. I guess that was half the problem.'

She glanced at him swiftly. 'With Arlene, you mean?'

'That's right.' There was nothing in his tone to suggest he objected to this line of discussion. 'Every night was party night. I couldn't stand the pace. Not with work, too.'

'So she started going alone?' Nicola hazarded. 'Couldn't you have stopped her?'

The smile had an element of irony. 'Short of locking her up every time I was out of town, no. What I should have done is ditched her. Let's speed it up, shall we? It's going to be dark before we get back.'

Nicola followed suit as he urged his mount into a canter, too immersed in her thoughts to worry about falling off. By his own admission, he hadn't loved his wife, yet he hadn't attempted to dissolve the marriage. It didn't make sense.

One thing she was sure of was the way she felt about him. That there was probably no future in it was something she had to face. When the time came to say goodbye they must, but for now she was going to make the most of what they had.

Supper was another of Maria's *paellas*. Afterwards, they played records on the old wind-up gramophone, laughing over the strange sounds emerging when the mechanism ran down. Maria withdrew discreetly to the rear quarters after clearing away, closing the connecting door with a smiling, meaningful glance over one comfortable shoulder.

'She thinks we're lovers,' Ross murmured softly, watching Nicola's face. 'Maybe it's time we lived up to our image.'

Her heart was thudding against her ribcage, her whole body tingling. 'Here?' she whispered.

'No, not here.' He was smiling. He came over to where she sat, drawing her unresistingly to her feet and holding her there in front of him to look into her eyes. 'I want to take you to bed, Nicola.'

'It isn't even nine o'clock,' she said, and saw the smile widen.

'So it's going to be a long night. Getting cold feet?'

She shook her head, going up on her toes to press her lips to his. 'I want you,' she said fiercely. 'Does that answer the question?'

He picked her up and carried her through to the bedroom—her bedroom. Watching him stripping off his clothing, she could only think how fine his body was, so lean and smoothly muscled, the skin unblemished. When he took her in his arms, it was as if her whole life had been geared towards this moment in time.

His lovemaking was all she had anticipated—all she could have hoped for. He didn't rush her, kissing her from stillness into quivering awareness of her own sensuality, drawing her on to respond in kind. There was no need for words, no need for anything beyond his tangible emotion. The way it should be, she thought mistily, abandoning herself to her body's demands: two people totally in tune with each other. She wanted to give him so much—to make up for all the agony of mind he had suffered in the past. When they slid together it was a union of earth-shattering moment, a climax that took her over the brink into a whole new world.

Awakening with that strong, warm body by her side was an experience in itself. Nicola lay motionless for several minutes, gazing at the features revealed by the dawn light. Odd to think that just over a week ago she hadn't even known this man existed. No, not quite true, she *had* known of his existence; what she could never have anticipated was finding herself in this situation. She could find no element of regret in her soul-searching. What she felt for Ross went far beyond the deep-down restrictions instilled by her mother over the years. Eight days was long enough to know one's own heart—even if she had spent two of them on the verge of consciousness.

He stirred restlessly, as if somehow aware of her scrutiny, opening his eyes to look directly into hers.

'Hi,' he said softly. 'Sleep well?'

She nodded, suddenly shy of him. They had shared an intimacy her body even now recalled with a tremor.

In the cold light of day, he might well regret the fact himself.

'Sorry now?' he asked with a tilt of a lip.

'No.' She could say that with certainty at least. 'I wanted you to make love to me, Ross.'

He smiled a little and kissed the end of her nose. 'No more than I did. You're a lovely, warm, wonderful creature, Nicola Sanderson! Did you know that?'

'No,' she said, snuggling closer. 'But keep on telling me!'

There was a spark in the grey eyes. 'I can show you better.'

She made no protest when Ross drew the covering sheet away from her, thrilling to the look in his eyes as he studied her shape. Hers was no voluptuous starlet's figure, but it seemed to please him. Her breasts fitted the palms of his hands as if made for them. The shuddering grew from inside her as he moved his thumbs gently over her nipples. She seized his wrists, wanting the touch, yet unable to bear it. He laughed, and bent to put his lips to the same place, his tongue a torment in its flickering passage.

He was too experienced for her; Nicola knew that already. But she could learn. She released her grasp in order to run her hands over the strong back, tracing the muscular structure of his shoulders with a feather-like lightness, moving on down the length of his spine to follow the firm curve of buttock, hearing the swift catch of his breath as she trailed her fingers across the hard male hipbone. He was everything she had ever dreamed of in a man; everything any woman might dream of. For the moment he was hers, but only for the moment. She must bear that in mind.

This time he made it last, intent, it seemed, on pleasing her as much as himself. At no point did he lose control; it was left to Nicola to do that. Wrapped in his arms, she fell asleep again afterwards, the smile on her lips an echo of the bliss in her heart.

He was gone when she awoke for the second time. The sun was already high enough to raise heat mist from the trees. She washed and dressed swiftly in a bright cotton skirt and blouse from her rejuvenated wardrobe, sliding her feet into raffia mules. There wasn't much point in using make-up in this climate; it simply slid off again. A quick dash of lipstick was her only concession.

She found Ross already eating breakfast on the veranda. In the full light of day she was hard put to keep a cool head as she met the grey eyes.

'Had a good sleep?' he remarked.

'You already asked me that once,' she reminded him, then blushed fiercely as memory caught up.

Amusement widened his lips, but there was no malice in the smile. 'Have some coffee.'

Nicola sat down, reaching for the coffee-pot with a hand that was creditably steady. Difficult to believe she had made love so passionately just a couple of hours ago with the man seated opposite. It had been wonderful, though; she felt her body stir afresh at the very thought.

'How long do you think it will be before Carlos gets back?' she queried.

'You've asked *me* that before.' His tone was light. 'I can only give you the same answer—I don't know.'

'How long has he been gone?'

'Nearly five weeks.' Ancipating her next question, he added, 'He said a month.'

So he was overdue. She said slowly, 'You don't think anything's happened to him?'

'It's always possible. Though I think they'd have contacted Santa Elena before now.'

'Unless he was caught in the floods.'

'In which case, it's too late anyway.' He shook his head at the expression in her eyes. 'It's the way Carlos would look at it himself.'

'Tell me about him.' she begged. 'What kind of a man is he?'

'The kind you can put your trust in, and they're few and far between.'

'Not so far between.' Her voice was soft.

His eyes kindled suddenly. He reached across to take her hand, turning it over to gently smooth the palm with his thumb. 'Nicola . . .'

Maria's arrival with the food forestalled what he had been about to say. She gave them both the benefit of her widest smile, obviously approving of what she saw. Ross let go of Nicola's hand and sat back in his chair to receive his loaded plate, leaving her to fight frustration the best way she could.

She waited a couple of minutes after the house-keeper's departure before saying tentatively, 'What were you going to tell me, Ross?'

He didn't look up. 'It wasn't important.'

She had a feeling it might be, to her, but she could hardly force him to say it. Whatever it was, he had obviously thought better of it.

Despite the rising heat, she ate a good breakfast. Sex must be good for the appetite, she reflected. But it wasn't just sex she had shared with Ross. It went so much deeper. The man revealed to her these past few days was far removed from the case-hardened stranger who had picked her up from that jungle track. Exactly how deeply his own emotions were involved it was still difficult to be sure. More than lust for certain, but how much more?

'So what do you want to do today?' he asked when Nicola pushed the empty plate away, mouth quirking at the sudden run of colour under her skin. 'Not practical—on my side, at any rate. Flattering, though. Unless you don't have much grounds for comparison.'

The colour came again. 'Are you asking me how

many other men I've slept with?'

Amusement was replaced by something less easily defined. 'It's none of my business.'

'I want it to be,' she insisted. 'There's only been the one before you.'

'Moral codes, or lack of opportunity?' He shook his head, mouth curling in self-deprecation. 'Forget I said that. I've lived too long in the wrong places.'

'We were planning on getting married,' she said after a moment, eyes on the liquid in her cup. 'Only it fell through.'

'Your choice, or his?'

'Mutual agreement. We'd no money, no jobs—no future.'

'Another actor?'

'Would-be.' Her smile was wry. 'I'm not the only one to find it difficult.'

'Not by a long way.' He was quiet for a moment, studying her. 'Were you serious when you said you weren't even sure about the vocation any more.?'

'Yes.' The shrug was defensive. 'I just don't have what it takes to make it.'

'If you feel that way, then I agree, you don't.' He paused again. 'So what else might you think of doing?'

'Anything else I'm qualified to do, I suppose. Not that it amounts to much.'

'Don't run yourself down,' Ross admonished. 'You're too intelligent to be stuck for long.'

Her laugh held irony. 'Not intelligent enough to recognise a set-up as obvious as that one the other day must have been!'

'You were under considerable strain at the time. It could have happened to anyone in those circumstances. And you escaped.'

'I'd have been captured again if wasn't for you.'

Lean features hardened a fraction. 'Was it gratitude that got you into bed with me?'

'No!' She said it swiftly, emphatically, eyes blazing blue. 'And if you don't know better than that, then you haven't learned anything about me!'

'I've learned one thing,' said Ross on a softer note. 'That I'd need to go a long way to find your equal—in any sphere. Now, tell me what you'd like to do today.'

The lump in the throat made it difficult to answer. Not a declaration of love exactly, but as close to it as he would probably ever come. She loved him; she could acknowledge it now. If only things had been different.

They went riding again when the day began to cool. Maria watched them depart, a look of satisfaction on her broad face.

'Do you think she suspects we spent the night together?' asked Nicola when they were clear of the yard.

'Probably.' Ross sounded unperturbed. 'She's been after finding me a woman since I got here.'

Something tautened ominously in her chest. 'She obviously thought you needed someone.'

'Not then, I didn't. It was the last thing I needed.' His tone shortened a little. 'Can we find some other subject?'

'You're right, of course,' she retorted with sudden frigidity. 'None of it has anything to do with me!'

She dug her heels in her mount's sides, causing him to leap forward into a canter. Ross caught up before they reached the river, seizing her rein to bring her to a halt.

'That was foolish,' he remonstrated. 'You could have come off. I wasn't telling you to mind your own business, just asking you to leave it alone for a while.'

'I know.' She was already ashamed of the outburst. 'You want to forget, and I won't let you.'

'You helped me get it into perspective,' he said. 'I'll not forget that.' He leaned over to pull her closer, planting a kiss on her upturned mouth. 'You're good for me, Nicola. More than you'll ever know.'

So tell me, she thought desperately as he moved on ahead.

By tacit consent, they avoided Santa Elena, choosing instead the narrow trails leading south. Ross carried a rifle strapped to his saddle for emergencies, although he had never been called on to use it, he had said. The wildlife in these parts was wary of man. Apart from the multi-hued birds, the occasional glimpse of a monkey, there was little enough on view. Filtered by the trees, the sun itself was just a vague golden glow.

The sight of the Land Rover standing outside the house on their return meant little at first, beyond the suggestion that Ramón must have had it out. It was only on coming closer that Nicola realised this vehicle had a different registration.'

'Carlos is back,' Ross said flatly, confirming her guess and sending her heart plummeting.

'*Two* Land Rovers,' was all she could find to say.

'The other's mine,' he returned. 'I bought it in Caracas to come down here.'

She said huskily, 'How is he going to react when he knows about . . . us?'

'If he's been here longer than a couple of minutes, Maria will already have told him the details, so we'll find out when we see him.' His glance was cursory. 'He had to come back some time.'

Yes, she *had* known that. She had even tried to prepare herself for the event. She should be thankful for Carlos's sake that he hadn't been caught in the floods, she reflected. This was his home, not Ross's—and certainly not hers.

The man who awaited them in the living-room was as dark as Ross, but much more swarthy of skin. Stocky in build, he was wearing a lightweight suit in which he had apparently travelled, to judge from its creased appearance.

'The wanderers return,' he greeted them in excellent, only slightly accented English. 'I've been waiting an hour or more to meet our new guest!'

Seeing the twinkle in the black eyes, Nicola felt the tension in her relax a little. 'I'm Nicola Sanderson,' she said diffidently. 'I imagine you already know why I'm here?'

His glance went from her face to that of the man at her back. 'Maria's version, yes.'

'It should be close enough,' Ross sounded offhand. 'How was the trip?'

The shrug was expressive. 'As anticipated. It's good to be home again.' He paused a moment before adding softly, 'And you, my friend? How comes the script?'

'Finished.' The younger man was moving as he spoke. 'Anyone else want a drink?'

Carlos lifted an enquiring eyebrow in Nicola's direction, saying when she shook her head, 'I'll have a whisky with you. To Nicola, he added, 'Shall we sit down? It's been a long and tiring journey.'

Ross brought the two glasses across, handing over the one and remaining standing himself. 'You came straight through?'

'Of course. The roads have been clear for several days now.' Carlos gave a sly little smile. 'Or didn't you notice that the rain had stopped?'

Grey eyes revealed no flicker of discomfiture. 'Sure.'

He was checking on the route out, thought Nicola dully. Until Carlos got back had been the original arrangement. There was no reason to suppose anything had changed. She caught Carlos watching her, and tried to conceal her emotions. It wouldn't do for either of them to guess how she was really feeling at this moment—Ross least of all. They had enjoyed a brief interlude of companionship, that was the way she must learn to look at it. Loving a man was one thing, eliciting the same emotion in him quite another. She would never forget him, that much she could say with certainty. If she could believe that her presence had in some small way helped to bring him back to life again, then it would be something.

The subject of her thoughts tossed back his whisky in a couple of gulps, and put down the glass. 'I'm for a shower,' he announced. 'Give you two chance to get acquainted.'

To what purpose? Nicola wondered, watching him stride from the room. Looking back at the man opposite, she felt tongue-tied. What was she supposed to say? What might he want to hear? She was here without invitation—an intruder in his home. Ross might be able to view the situation with equanimity; she couldn't.

'I'm sorry,' she said at length. 'You must be thinking of me in the worst possible terms.'

'Why should I do that?' His tone was mild. 'According to what Maria tells me, you've made Ross very happy while you've been here. For that I should thank you, not condemn you. He needed to be taken out of himself. He was a man too much involved in the past.'

'How did the two of you meet?' she asked after a moment.

'In Caracas, some years ago. He was on location.'

'And you've kept in touch ever since?'

'From time to time. I'm very proud that he chose to come to me in his time of trouble. He knew that here he wouldn't be disturbed by the media.'

'I suppose not.' She hesitated before voicing the thought. 'I more than half expected you to be an older man yourself, living so far away from everything like this.'

He smiled. 'By everything, you mean the so-called civilised world?'

'Well . . . yes.'

'One month a year is all I need to have my fill of the

fleshpots. El Milagro is where I'm happiest.'

'You don't miss having a wife and family here with you?'

'I've yet to meet the woman who would be content with the life I lead here.' The dark eyes were quizzical. 'Would you?'

She kept her tone light. 'Probably not.'

'But then you don't have to,' he said. 'Ross will be ready soon to return to his homeland.'

Nicola swallowed on the sudden lump in her throat. 'We don't have any permanent arrangement. In fact, I'll most likely be leaving myself in the morning.'

'Because I came back?' He sounded surprised. 'There's no need, I assure you. You're welcome to stay as long as you like.'

'I doubt if it's going to be up to me,' she acknowledged. 'I knew what I was getting into. I can hardly start complaining now. My mother would have said it was all I merited.'

'You are not your mother,' Carlos rejoined. 'And I doubt if this kind of affair is one you often indulge in. Ross underwent an experience he isn't likely to forget in a hurry. It will take time and patience to convince him into believing wholly in anyone again. I think you could be the one to do it—if you feel enough for him.'

'What I feel for him isn't the point,' she declared. 'I just happened to turn up at a time when he was beginning to need a woman again. But basically that's all I am to him.'

'How can you be sure?' Carlos insisted. 'Has he said you have to leave?'

'Not yet. There's hardly been time.'

'Then at least wait and see. Give him the opportunity to think about it.'

It wasn't going to make any difference, she thought dully, recalling the change in him when he had seen the Land Rover outside. She had been deluding herself in imagining he felt anything for her that really mattered. It would be both easier and face-saving if she announced her own departure. He might insist on driving her to Caracas, but he would probably be relieved to have the matter taken out of his hands.

Carlos shrugged when she made no reply. 'You know your own mind best.' He added curiously, 'I'd be interested to hear how you came to be so far from the regular tourist centres yourself.'

'It's a long story,' she said, and set out to tell it.

He listened without comment, other than a nod or a frown here and there. Only when she reached the end of the tale did he say succinctly, 'You were fortunate.' There was a brief pause. 'You say you're an actress?'

It was Nicola's turn at the philosophical shrug. 'Aspiring to be. It's an overcrowded profession.'

'So I understand.' His eyes were on the glass in his hand. 'Perhaps Ross might be of some help.'

'No!' The negative was too forceful, drawing his glance. Flushing a little, she made some attempt to temper her reaction. 'That isn't the reason I stayed with him. I'm not sure I have any ambition left in that direction.'

'It's called disillusionment,' said Ross from the archway. 'Comes to us all in time.'

'Some sooner than others,' returned their host smoothly. 'How was the hot water?'

'Still coming when I left it.' Ross took a seat on the same sofa Nicola was using, crossing one leg comfortably over the other. 'Talking of leaving, I think it's time I went home myself.'

It was a moment or two before Carlos replied. When he did speak, it was levelly. 'If you feel that way, then you're right. When did you have in mind?'

'Tomorrow. There's no point in prolonging things.' The glance he sent in Nicola's direction was fleeting. 'Can you be ready that soon?'

She nodded, not trusting her voice. Killing two birds with one stone, she thought achingly. And why not? As he had said himself, there was no point in prolonging things any further.

They left soon after dawn. Carlos was awake to see them off, the only farewell between the two men a firm handshake and an exchange of glances.

'I had little opportunity to know you,' the Venezuelan said to Nicola as Ross preceded her out to the waiting car, 'but I wish you luck for the future. Perhaps,' he added with a smile, 'I may even see your name in newsprint one day.'

'Stranger things have happened,' she agreed lightly. 'Goodbye, Carlos—and thanks.'

He spread his hands, mouth wry. 'For what?'

Ross was already behind the wheel with the engine running. He scarcely waited for her to close the passenger door before putting the vehicle into motion. It was left to Nicola herself to turn in her seat and wave to the man standing on the veranda. Then they were out of the gate and the trees were closing about them, hiding the house from sight.

'How can he bear it?' she said, thinking her thoughts out loud. 'It has to be lonely!'

'If he found it so bad, he wouldn't choose to live that way,' Ross responded briefly. 'Don't worry about it.'

It was none of her concern; she had to agree with that. Her own future looked less than bright right now. Better, perhaps, when she was actually on the plane home to England and could start putting all this behind her. She might never forget it, but she could learn to live with the memories. When it came right down to it, she had no other choice.

'How long will it take us to reach Caracas?' she asked, trying for a practical note.

'About four hours—providing we don't run into any hold-ups.' He changed down to take the ford, and added reasonably, 'Why don't you get some sleep? There might not be too much chance later on.'

Meaning, if he could get seats on afternoon or evening flights, he would do it, reckoned Nicola. By this time tomorrow, she could well be back on home ground again. It was hardly Ross's fault if she viewed that prospect with little enthusiasm.

He had not come to her room last night. She hadn't really expected him to. While not retreating into the cold shell, he was staying aloof, keeping her at a distance. Whatever these last few days had meant to him, it was over. He had his life to lead, she had hers.

Regardless, she couldn't find it in herself to regret any part of their time together. Meeting Ross had brought her a new maturity—a realisation of what loving a man really meant. She hadn't loved Barry. Not in the same way. Had they married, she might never have known the despair she was feeling at this moment, but neither would she have experienced the heights to which Ross had lifted her. No pleasure without pain, wasn't that what they said?

She dozed eventually, wakening again, stiff and disorientated, to find the Land Rover halted at some wayside petrol station. They had left the forest belt and were out on the cultivated prairie land, south of the capital. Another hour and a half, she calculated with a glance at her watch, and they would reach their destination. What Ross intended doing with the car, she had no idea. Certainly, he wouldn't be taking it with him. It had to be worth several thousand pounds on the open market. More than enough, she thought with an edge of cynicism, to see her on her way.

He got back into the car, glancing her way before starting the engine. 'Hungry?'

Nicola shook her head. 'I can wait till we get to Caracas.'

'Maybe as well. This place doesn't have much to

offer.' He fired the ignition, sliding smoothly into first gear. 'Another hour or so and we'll be there. First thing is to get rid of this, then we'll find an agency to fix tickets.'

'You don't waste any time,' she murmured, and drew a faint smile.

'I've done enough of that these past months.'

She was silent, not trusting her voice too much. He had everything mapped out, it was evident. The past was behind him. If she had helped him put it there, she could only be glad.

Caracas was reached mid-morning. Driving along the wide and lovely boulevards, Nicola could only wish that she was seeing the city under happier circumstances. There had been no time for anything beyond a fleeting glimpse on the incoming journey—how long ago that seemed! Her South American adventure had proved rather more than she could comfortably handle in the end.

Ross pulled in at the first used car dealers they saw, accepting the price offered without argument. Piling their respective suitcases into the cab summoned by the salesman, he asked to be taken to the nearest travel agency—or at least that was what Nicola assumed he said. It took no more than two minutes, anyway. Left sitting in the vehicle while he went inside the building, she spent the time watching the passing traffic and listening to the driver's cheerfully tuneless whistle, stifling the growing urge to yell at him to shut up.

Ross was back in what seemed like only moments. The grey eyes gave nothing away.

''*Consulate Americano*,' he commanded the driver. '*Pronto!*'

Nicola didn't look at him as he slid into the seat beside her. 'Having trouble?' she asked thickly.

'Nothing that can't be sorted, with a bit of luck.' There was an odd note to his voice. 'We have roughly three hours to fix the paperwork and get out to the airport. There's an LA flight at two.'

The breath caught suddenly in her throat. She stared at him, unable to believe what her senses were telling her. 'I'm not sure I understand,' she got out.

'I bought two tickets to LA,' he said. 'There's a London flight out tonight if you'd rather say goodbye now.' He studied her face, his smile hinting just a fraction of cynicism. 'If I'm taking too much for granted, just say so.'

Nicola was glad of the closed anti-mugging partition between them and the driver. She felt dazed. 'Why wait till now?' she heard herself asking. 'We just spent four hours on the road!'

'I wasn't sure enough of you to give you too much time to think about it,' he said. 'This seemed the best way.' He made no attempt to touch her. 'I want to take you back with me, Nicola.'

'As what?' The anger and pain were mingled inextricably. 'Your mistress?'

'My wife.' His lips twisted at the sudden darkening of her eyes. 'It won't be any picnic, I realise that. The media will go to town on it. I know you feel something for me. Is it enough?'

It took every bit of control she had to damp down her instinctive reaction, to say softly, 'It takes more than one.'

Something flickered deep down in the grey eyes, gone before she could put a name to it. 'If you're asking me do I love you, I'd have thought the answer obvious.'

She wanted to laugh suddenly at the memory of all the misery she had endured these past hours. Hysteria, she told herself. Sheer hysteria! 'How can someone with your gift for sensitive directing be so completely obtuse?' she demanded. 'How was I supposed to know unless you said it? What am I, a mind reader?'

His face relaxed. 'So I placed too much trust in

feminine intuition. To me, it seemed obvious.' He put out a hand and cupped her chin, smoothing a thumb over her lower lip. 'You're everything Arlene wasn't. How could I help but love you? From the moment you stepped out in front of the car that night, I was on my way up again.'

'It didn't show.' Her voice was low, her eyes like twin sapphires. 'I despaired of ever getting through that armour. Ross, are you sure this is what you want?'

'Couldn't be surer.'

The kiss sealed it for her. He couldn't pretend to an emotion like that. He had no reason for pretence, anyway. Why even suspect it?

'Three hours', she murmured against his chest. 'Can we do it?'

'We're not going to try.' His voice was roughened. 'I'll change the tickets, take a couple of days here—do the thing properly. It's been a year; a little longer isn't going to hurt.'

Nicola felt relief flood through her. She needed time, not to make up her mind, but to assimilate this new development. Ross's wife! Much as she loved him, she knew it wasn't going to be easy. As he had said, the media alone would make sure of that. But she could face it. They could both face it. Ross had a career to go back to, she had a new one to start. This was one marriage that was going to succeed.

The contract was signed and sealed the following afternoon, the witnesses duly rewarded. Emerging once more into the hot sunlight, Nicola wondered why she felt no different. Last night they had slept together as two single people; could a mere change of name improve on what they already had? Mrs Ross King. It sounded so strange.

Their hotel was large and luxurious and catered to every need. Ross had booked a suite looking towards the Cerro de Avila. From the balcony one could see the cablecars ascending and descending, catch a glimpse of the white tower at the summit when the drifting clouds obliged. There were two bedrooms, two superbly equipped bathrooms, a sitting-room big enough to hold a ball in, even a tiny kitchenette for the guest who fancied a little self-help.

Too much, Nicola had thought on first sighting. They could have managed perfectly well with an ordinary double room. Ross hadn't worked in more than a year. No matter what his earnings had been in the past, that had to have had some effect on his financial bearing.

Yet if there was cause for concern he wasn't acknowledging it. He had taken her out yesterday and insisted she replenish her wardrobe. Considering where she was going to be living, she had been unable to argue with that expense. Some of her own things she was keeping, the rest she had given to the maids who daily serviced the suite. Poorly paid, the latter were grateful for any gift, be it money, clothing, cosmetics, even soap. The comparison between their home environment and this must be ludicrous, Nicola thought, but it seemed to matter little to them.

The dress she had worn for the wedding was blue. Like her eyes, Ross had said when he'd chosen it. In the pale grey suit, he looked a different man. Only when he took her in his arms and kissed her did the strangeness begin to dissolve. Husband and wife, she thought joyfully, exultantly. Mr *and* Mrs Ross King!

CHAPTER FIVE

THE King homestead was reached via a winding canyon road, affording superb views at every bend. Pure modern Californian in design, the house itself was built on several different levels to follow the contours of the mountainside on which it stood, protected from the passing public by stone walls and double iron gates.

Ross got out of the cab to open a small box set into one of the gateposts and take out what looked like a telephone receiver. He spoke rapidly into it for a moment, then replaced the instrument, coming back to regain his seat as the gates swung smoothly and silently open.

'Cosy little place, isn't it?' he commented, drawing up before the wide frontage of one-way glass.'

Nicola stayed silent, not yet sure enough of herself to make any judgements. The first-class flight here, the obvious recognition of Ross's name both by the cabin staff and the receiving officer on immigration, the city itself, so huge and confusing—none of it helped. She was out of her depth by a mile and a half, and it showed.

One portion of the glass opened to reveal a woman in her mid to late forties, clad in a pale lilac dress. Her dark hair was beautifully groomed, her make-up expertly applied. The smile on her lips failed to reach her eyes, Nicola noted, following Ross out of the cab.

'It's good to have you home again, Mr King,' the woman said smoothly. 'You should have let us know you were coming. Judd would have brought the car to pick you up.'

'It was a sudden decision,' Ross returned, ignoring the implied criticism. 'Nicola, this is Mrs Graham.' The pause was brief enough to be almost non-existent. 'My wife.'

The older woman retained her smile as he turned back to pay off the cab-driver, though her eyes had registered shock. Her swift and comprehensive survey belied any welcome. Nicola felt weighed up and found deficient in every sphere. Oddly enough, that knowledge served to put her on her mettle. No doubt she hardly matched up to the Hollywood standard of beauty, but she was Ross's choice. She would stand no patronising from this woman.

'How do you do?' she said politely.

The cab was already on the move again, scrunching the gravel as it turned in a wide sweep to head back down the drive. Deposited alongside Ross's supple, well travelled leather, her suitcase looked glaringly new. The clothes inside them were for the most part unworn. The suit in which she had travelled was Italian, woven from a mixture of silk and cotton in a shade of cream she would have considered totally impractical back home. It had cost the earth, but it made her feel like a million dollars. Fine feathers make fine birds, she reminded herself with irony.

'Judd will be out in a moment,' said the housekeeper, as Ross bent to lift a bag in each hand. 'He was in the grounds when you rang.'

'No problem,' returned her employer. 'I can manage.' His smile was directed at Nicola. 'Lead the way.'

She did so, to find herself in a huge light area in which plantlife proliferated. The ground floor was built on the open-plan design, with steps and archways providing the only division between rooms. From where she stood, Nicola could see through to where a whole wall of glass gave on to a wide terrace and swimming pool. On another level, off to the right, an inset pool discharged a waterfall, which in turn fed a second, lower pool complete with flowering lilies and fish.

Ross watched her face as she took it all in, a sardonic tilt to his mouth. 'You haven't seen anything yet!'

Nicola had seen enough already to know why he had no feeling for this place he called home. It was like something out of one of those glossy magazines; soulless was the word she would have applied. If not his own choice, then it had to have been Arlene's. Love her or not, he had obviously been able to deny her little. One had to be talking in the hundreds of thousands when it came to real estate in this part of the world.

'Which room will you be using?' asked Mrs Graham from the rear. 'I'll need a little time to prepare.'

'South side, I think,' said Ross, dropping both suitcases to the floor. 'And can you rustle us up something to eat? A sandwich will do. We'll be on the terrace.'

He took Nicola's arm to lead the way, the pressure reassuring. Whatever material the floor was made of, it wasn't marble, she realised at once when their footsteps failed to make more than the faintest sound. The furnishings were pure space-age; wildly expensive, she had no doubt, but lacking warmth and welcome. It took the golden light of the Californian sunshine to create that impression. There was a panoramic view over the city, the smog line like a skid mark along the horizon.

'Better?' asked Ross at her shoulder as she stood at the balustrade, drinking in the scene. 'I'd forgotten just how depressing the place was!'

'If you dislike it so much,' Nicola murmured diffidently, 'perhaps you should think about selling it.'

'Always providing I can find a buyer.'

'If the price is right, there's always a buyer.'

'You could be right at that.' He ran a finger down her

nape, added softly, 'Sorry you came?'

With his touch still tingling her skin, the answer was immediate and easy. 'Of course not.'

'Good.' He moved away from her to take off his jacket and sling it over a lounger. 'Want a drink?'

She started to shake her head, then abruptly changed her mind. 'Something long and cool, please.'

There was a walk-in bar built into a side wall. Ross filled two tall glasses with ice-cubes taken from some store beneath the counter-top, poured measures from a couple of bottles into each and topped up from a third.

'Will the refrigerator have been running since you left?' asked Nicola on a bemused note when he brought the drinks across to where she had taken a seat.

He looked blank for a moment, then shrugged. 'I don't imagine the ice is that old.'

It wasn't the age of the ice she had been thinking of. If Mrs Graham had been running the house as normal for the past year, the accumulated bills were surely going to be enormous! As Ross seemed unconcerned by any such thought, she could only assume that her fears regarding his financial status were groundless. This was a different world from the one she was used to, she reminded herself drily. High-income people were usually pretty shrewd when it came to investments—or their advisors were.

The drink tasted good. She didn't bother to ask what was in it. Mrs Graham came out, carrying a loaded tray, depositing plates and coffee-pots on the nearest of the low tables. The American version of a sandwich was in the nature of a full meal, the single round of rye bread piled high with wafer-thin slices of cooked beef and surrounded by salad. The aroma was mouth-watering.

'I'm preparing the guest suite,' declared the house-keeper expressionlessly. 'Is that all right with you, Mr King?'

'Sounds fine,' agreed Ross, already laying into his

sandwich.

Why the guest suite? Nicola was about to ask, then bit her tongue as realisation hit her. Ross would probably want to be as far away as possible from the room or rooms he had shared with his wife. It seemed likely that the guest suite would be on the opposite side of the house. A tremor ran through her at the thought of sharing a bed with him. Hardly the first time, of course, but it felt strange all the same. The difference being that, back in Venezuela, they had both of them been in neutral territory, while here he was on home ground.

There was so much more to the whole situation than she had allowed herself to think about in depth this past couple of days. As Ross's wife, she could hardly remain aloof from the people he knew—the people who had known Arlene. She knew enough about the public appetite for scandal to realise that all hell was likely to break loose once the media got wind of his return with a new young wife. Speculation would be rife, her feelings the last consideration. At least with the security system in operation here there was little chance of any news-hound reaching the house. That was some small comfort.

Mrs Graham was not in evidence when they eventually made their way up the open staircase. Corridors branching right and left held more doors than Nicola could count at a glance. The guest suite had its own sitting-room in addition to bed and bath, the whole decorated in shades of apricot and white and sumptuously furnished. The bed was a brass four-poster draped in filmy sheers.

'Lovely,' she commented automatically, wondering how she could possibly live up to such surroundings. 'And look at that view!'

'The same one you saw downstairs.' Ross pointed out. He turned her towards him, looking down at her with a smile in his eyes. 'I prefer this view.'

She responded with reticence when he kissed her, still too much the stranger here to relax. He released her without comment, his voice casual as he said, 'I'm for a shower. Want to join me?'

She said swiftly, 'I have to unpack.'

Already moving away, he spoke over a shoulder. 'I'd guess Mrs Graham already did that for us both. Take a look.'

Nicola waited until the door had closed behind him before moving the width of the room to the dressing area containing a whole wall of wardrobes and drawers. New and old, the contents of her suitcase looked miserably inadequate among the row of empty hangers. A second wardrobe was full of suits—she counted twenty—while yet another held sports and casual wear. It still left one empty. Arlene could probably have filled it twenty times over, came the thought. For herself, it was going to be necessary to enlist some help. She had to look the part, even if she didn't feel it.

Ross was wearing a white towelling robe when he emerged from the bathroom. His hair was damp, curling a little at the ends.

'I've a couple of calls to make,' he said. 'Take your time.'

He sounded a little abrupt. Nicola wondered if it was because she had refused to take a shower with him. Different room or no, she felt restricted by the very knowledge that Arlene had shared his days and nights in the same house. How could he not compare the two of them in these surroundings?

Needing time to relax and think, she ran water into the sunken bath, throwing in a generous handful of fragrant salts. The walls were all mirror glass; she could see herself reflected from every angle. The lighting made her skin look golden, her hair like spun silk. Land of illusion, she thought with an edge of cynicism.

She had been lying in the warm, fragrant water for

several minutes when Ross came into the room.

'Nice,' he said appreciatively as she jerked upright. 'You look like a startled nymph!'

'I never had a man walk in on me in the bath before,' she rejoined. 'Did you finish your calls?'

'The essential ones, yes. We're invited to a party tonight. Sam Walker. He's head of Magnum Studios.'

Nicola stared at him, forgetful of her nudity for the moment. 'So soon?'

'We have to face it some time,' he said. 'Might as well be sooner as later.'

'You told him about . . . . us?'

He gave her a thoughtful look. 'I can hardly keep you a secret! What are you afraid of?'

She drew a deep, steadying breath. 'Everything! I need time, Ross.' She attempted to laugh. 'I'm not even used to being married yet!'

'That's something you can do in private; this is something we both need to do in public.'

'Not tonight,' she appealed desperately. 'Ross, I can't. It's too soon! If you have to go, can't you go alone?'

A line appeared between the dark brows. 'I could, but I'm not going to. You're an actress. It shouldn't be too difficult a part to play.'

'You don't put anyone centre-stage without adequate rehearsal,' she came back. 'You're expecting too much.'

There was a pause, a sudden softening of expression. 'You're right, I am. Why shouldn't I keep you to myself for a while?'

He came up the step on to the low dais in which the bath was set, bending to slide his hands beneath her armpits and lift her bodily from the water, totally disregarding the wetness seeping though his robe as he kissed her long and hard.

Desire rose in her, swift and sweet, bringing her up on her toes the better to reach him. She felt his hands cradling her hips as he brought her to him, the pulsating surge of his own need. Then he was swinging her up in his arms, bearing her down to level ground to lay her on the thickly piled carpet, slipping off his robe before coming over her. For the first time that day, Nicola felt the doubts and fears fade from her mind, replaced by a deeper, more certain emotion as their bodies joined—became one. Whatever Ross had been in the past, whatever he might become in the future, she loved him now, this minute, as no man had ever been loved before.

It was a long time afterwards before she was capable of thinking clearly again. They had progressed from the bathroom to the bed, lying replete in each other's arms as day turned into night. Ross was the first to stir, albeit with reluctance.

'If I'm going to make my entry, I'd better prepare for it.'

'Do you really *have* to go?' she asked, already knowing the answer.

'If I want to work again. Sam has a screenplay he wants me to look at. He's been keeping it on ice since . . .' He broke off, jaw tensing a little. 'Anyway, it sounds right up my alley.'

'What about your own screenplay?' Nicola ventured. 'Isn't that the main reason you decided to come back?'

'The excuse, maybe.' There was a pause before he added levelly, 'You were right the first time. It was more of a therapy than anything. I don't plan on using it.'

Nicola put up a hand and touched his lips with her fingertips. 'Best not,' she agreed on soft note. 'It's behind you now, Ross—all of it. Let it stay there.'

He made a sound in his throat, half-way between a groan and a sigh, drawing her close again to kiss her temple. 'Don't change,' he murmured into her hair. 'Don't ever change!'

'I won't,' she promised, her heart overflowing. 'I wouldn't know how.'

He left the house alone at eight. Had he made any further attempt to persuade her to accompany him, Nicola knew she would not have been able to hold out, but he hadn't. She had to get this whole thing into perspective, she acknowledged ruefully, listening to the car engine fading into the distance. Ross needed a supportive partner, not a cringing little ninny! So people were going to talk, to speculate, to compare. Let them! She had his love, his name, his trust to back her. What more could she ask?

Mrs Graham came back around nine to collect the dinner tray Ross had ordered for her. Nicola had eaten and enjoyed every scrap of the beautifully prepared duck à l'orange. She said as much now, half anticipating the other's total indifference. The housekeeper saw her as an interloper; she was making that all too clear. Nicola schooled herself not to care too much. Either the woman accepted the situation, or she and her husband found other jobs. She could run the house herself if it came to that.

She had not expected to sleep without Ross in the strange bed, but the first she knew of his return was when he slid in beside her in the darkness.

'Go back to sleep,' he murmured when she stirred.

'What time is it?' she asked, smothering a yawn. 'I waited up till gone one.'

'It's almost three.' An arm came over her waist, drawing her back to rest against him. 'I missed you tonight.'

Warmth curled through her. 'How did it go?'

'Predictably.' He sounded a little uptight. 'Few things change in this town.'

She rolled over on to her back, trying to see his features in the darkness. 'They gave you a bad time?'

'Not on the surface. That's all it is with most of

them—a veneer.'

'Sam Walker included?'

'No. He's one of the few. Sam gave me my first Hollywood job. I owe him a lot.'

She said softly, 'His faith was repaid.'

'Maybe, but it's that initial gamble that counts. I was a complete unknown out here.'

It wasn't the first time she had wondered about his background, just the first time she had felt able to ask. 'What made you decide to become a director?'

His hand had lifted to her breast, not moving, just holding her. 'Amateur dramatics in high school is where it started, I guess. That was back in Boston— more than twenty years ago.'

'You still have family there?'

'Not any more. Dad died when I was nine, my mother's had three husbands since. Latest one is an Australian.' He put his lips to the point of her shoulder, brushing them softly across her skin. 'If you're not going to sleep . . .'

Her arms were ready for him. 'I'm sorry I was such an idiot about tonight,' she murmured thickly.

His smile was just discernible. 'Who's complaining?'

Not her for one, she thought as his mouth found hers. Whatever she might have to endure, this made it worth while.

Life settled into a pattern of sorts over the following few days. Ross was out of the house by ten each morning, returning late afternoon, still mentally immersed in a world into which Nicola had no insight. It was a fairly low-budget film, with comparative unknowns in the leading roles, she learned, but it had box-office potential'.

'We'll be doing the studio shots first,' he said over breakfast on the terrace some five days after their arrival in California. 'That should take around three weeks, then another four on location up north. Guy's looking to bring it in by the end of January.'

Guy Grayling was the producer—a name with which Nicola was already acquainted through screen titles. She said carefully, 'He produced your last film, didn't he?'

'And the two before it.' There was no apparent alteration in tone. 'I think we've the makings of another success in *The Spoilers*. It's got the right ingredients. Not that there's any certainty till it hits the circuits.' He finished his coffee, added levelly, 'Sorry I've been so tied up. I didn't anticipate getting back into harness this quickly.'

'It doesn't matter,' Nicola lied. 'I preferred to lie low till the heat was off, anyway. At least they've stopped hanging around the front gate.'

'We're old news. There was nothing in *The Times* yesterday.' He sounded relatively unmoved. 'There may be another flare-up of interest when you make your first public appearance, but the worst is over. Svengali can do his manipulating in peace.'

Her laugh was just a little forced. 'That really was a bitch of an article!'

'Written by a bitch.' His lip curled cynically. 'And there are few more bitchy than Arlene was!' A shrug dismissed the subject. 'What would you like to do today?'

Her heart leapt. 'You don't have to go to the studio?'

'Not essentially. There's a detail or two still to sort out, but nothing that can't wait. Just say the word.'

Happiness flooded her, sparkling her eyes. 'I'd like the whole tourist bit,' she declared. 'All the places I've heard about—like the Hollywood Bowl, for instance, and Graumann's Chinese Theatre.'

'Mann's,' Ross corrected. 'It's just called Mann's these days.' He sounded resigned. 'I guess I asked for it.'

'You sure did!' She wrinkled her nose at him. 'It's a minor sacrifice.'

'You reckon?' His regard was indulgent. 'I'll need compensation.'

'As much as you like.'

'Now, there's an offer!' He got to his feet, running a hand over her hair in passing. 'Give me ten minutes to make a call.'

'That's all right,' she assured him. 'I'll need to change, anyway.'

A pair of her own slacks and a matching shirt would suffice for today's jaunt, she decided in the bedroom. They were unlikely to meet anyone who might know who Ross was on the tourist circuits. Not for the first time, she wished they were still at El Milagro. She might not have had Ross's ring on her finger, but at least they would have been free of the pressures that beset them here.

Ross made no comment on her appearance when she joined him outside at the car. He appeared abstracted. Probably still thinking about the film, Nicola told herself, trying not to let his lack of response detract too much from the occasion. He was stealing time to be with her. That was the main thing. She had to learn to take the rough with the smooth in more ways than one.

He loosened up during the course of the afternoon, tolerant of her naïve delight in things which were, to him so familiar. Strolling the length of Hollywood's Walk of Fame, where the greats of the entertainment industry were emblazoned in the pavement, matching hand and footprints with those etched in concrete outside Mann's Chinese Theatre, standing at the very top of the great curving hollow that was the Hollywood Bowl and looking up to see the world famous sign spelling out the name of the city in letters forty-five feet high—she enjoyed it all.

'I never learned how to be blasé,' she excused herself when they were back in the car and driving along Sunset Boulevard past the pink splendour of the

Beverly Hills Hotel. 'I've seen all this so many times in magazines or films, I just never expected to be here, that's all.'

Ross smiled. 'Don't apologise. It makes a refreshing change.'

She slanted a glance at the lean profile. 'Does it?'

'That's what the man said. If I'd wanted another sophisticate, I'd have put you on that plane back to Heathrow.' It was his turn to glance across. 'How much convincing do I have to do?'

There was just the faintest edge to his voice. Nicola bit her lip. He was right, she lacked confidence in herself. To a certain extent, if she were totally honest, she still lacked it in him. He might love her now, but would it last? That article the other day had done more than hint at his own infidelities.

He hadn't bothered to deny it, simply tossed the paper aside with an exclamation of disgust. If it was true, then perhaps there had been some excuse for Arlene's behaviour. By his own admittance, he hadn't loved her. She must have known it.

'Where are we going?' she asked, trying for a lighter note.

'Up the coast a bit,' he said. 'We can take a walk on the beach.'

'Sounds great!' Nicola really meant it. Later, when she was alone again, the uncertainties would return to plague her; for now, she was keeping them well damped down.

They drove out towards Malibu along the coastal highway, the scenery spectacular with its long stretches of golden sand backed by Pacific rollers. When Ross pulled into the driveway of a house fronting one of the beaches, Nicola was unable to conceal her dismay.

'I'm not dressed for visiting,' she protested. 'You should have warned me!'

'We're not visiting,' he said, cutting the engine. 'I

thought you might like to see the place.'

She gave him a swift glance. 'This is yours, too?'

He smiled a little. 'It was where I was living when I first met Arlene. I never got round to getting rid.'

'She didn't like it out here?'

'Out here was OK, the house wasn't. Too small and too old, to name but a few. She designed the other place. She and an architect friend of hers.'

One of her lovers? wondered Nicola fleetingly. Aloud she said, 'Is this the first time you've been back?'

'The first time I've felt like it,' he admitted. 'Want to go inside?'

She felt suddenly buoyant, uplifted by the knowledge that he had waited until she was with him to return to his old home. 'Of course!'

The front door opened straight into a wide hallway, from which arches on either side gave on to well proportioned living areas. The furnishings were dust-sheeted, the curtains semi-drawn over floor to ceiling windows. Sunlight flooded in when Ross pulled them back. There was a wide wooden deck outside, with steps leading down on to the beach itself. From here, the sea looked limitless in its blueness.

'It's lovely,' Nicola exclaimed softly. 'Just right!'

'It used to be.' He was looking out towards the water, eyes narrowed against the glare.

'It could be again.' She was trying hard not to sound over-eager. 'You hate where we're living now—why not move back here?'

His glance held appraisal. 'You'd like that?'

'It isn't up to me,' she insisted. 'It's what you want—where you feel most comfortable. I suppose the only drawback would be the distance from town.'

Ross laughed. 'Twenty miles is no great hassle.'

'Then you'd consider it?'

'Maybe.' Grey eyes took on a new expression. 'Do you fancy a swim?'

It was her turn to laugh. 'I don't have a suit with me.'

'No problem. There's sure to be something lying around upstairs.'

Her jaw contracted. 'Of Arlene's?'

'I guess so.' He didn't appear to have noted her inflection. 'She spent the occasional weekend out here.'

With whom? came the thought, swiftly discarded as of no consequence now. Arlene was in the past; she had to leave her there. So what did it matter who the swimsuit might have belonged to?

'Let's take a look,' she said on a light note.

The staircase gave on to a broad open landing, with doors leading off both sides. Ross opened the first one on the left to reveal a large room dust-sheeted like the ones down below, and dimmed by the slatted shutters over the windows. The carpet underfoot felt soft and springy to Nicola's tread. A faint perfume seemed to linger in the air—or was it in her mind? She shook off the sense of intrusion with an effort.

'Try the chest over there,' Ross invited, making for another draped shape closer to the windows. 'I know I left some trunks in here.'

The chest in question was made of solid mahogany, its drawers lined in a paler wood, smooth as satin to her fingertips. The first one she opened was half-full of silk underwear, carelessly tossed around, as if riffled through by an impatient hand. The same perfume tantilised her nostrils, emotively expensive. Nicola had a sudden picture in her mind of that darkly beautiful face and smouldering green eyes, the body so slender and yet so sensual. She closed the drawer again abruptly, doing the same with a second containing what appeared to be articles of nightwear.

It was almost a relief to find a couple of bikinis with matching wraps in a lower drawer, although they were both of them briefer than she would have chosen for herself. She selected the pale blue one, turning with it in her hand to find Ross watching her from across the room. He had stripped ready to don the trunks he held, but had not yet done so. His body was slatted in tiger stripes by the light filtering through the window shutters at his back, his face shadowed.

'We'll swim later,' he said thickly. 'I want you, Nicola.'

Her own voice sounded strange. 'Here?'

'And now.' He was moving towards her as he spoke, stirring her to life despite herself in his vibrant masculinity. 'I need to feel you with me.'

Laying his ghosts? she wondered with a cynicism of her own, but it made little difference to her responses. Need was a part of love—a very vital part.

Passion flared through her at his touch, sending her forwards into his arms, her mouth feverishly seeking. The practised ease with which he divested her of her clothing might once have meant something; right now, she was as eager as he was to know the tactile sensation of flesh against flesh, to have his hands exploring her body, to be possessed utterly and completely by this man she had married.

They made love slowly and deliciously, oblivious of the dust-sheets still covering the king-sized bed. Without air-conditioning, and with all the windows closed, it was hot in the room, slicking their bodies with perspiration. For Nicola, the taste of salt on her tongue was a stimulant in itself. She couldn't have enough of him, couldn't bear for this long and lovely afternoon to end. Even when, drained at last, she lay quiescent in his arms, the fire still smouldered deep down within, needing but a breath to fan it into flame again.

'Wonderwoman!' murmured Ross against her cheek. 'What happened to all that English reserve?'

'It gave way to American aggression!' She took the lobe of his ear between sharp teeth and nibbled, smiling at his indrawn breath. 'The sun's almost down.'

'And we still haven't taken that swim.' He rolled away from her to sit up, his features obscure in the dimmed light. 'There's time yet.'

The bikini was on the floor where she had dropped it. She didn't look his way as she drew it on. Arlene's breasts had been smaller than hers, she realised with some surprise. Yet on screen they had looked so voluptuous. So that was Hollywood, she reminded herself. Little was as it seemed.

Ross led the way downstairs again. It was cooler outside on the deck, with a faint breeze coming in off the sea. The sun was a soft golden globe touching the horizon. Darkness would be on them within minutes of its going down.

'Do you think we should?' she asked in sudden trepidation as he made for the steps leading down to the beach. 'What about sharks?'

His grin was unexpected. 'More on land than sea this stretch of the coast! Don't be faint-hearted. Life's nothing without taking a few risks.'

Always providing there was a fair chance of coming out on the winning side, reflected Nicola, driving herself forwards to join him.

CHAPTER SIX

THEY spent only ten minutes or so in the water, warm though it was. Returning up the beach, Ross's arm across her shoulders, Nicola felt at peace with the whole world. Even the darkness was friendly. There were other dwellings to either hand, some occupied, some unlit. When asked about his immediate neighbours, Ross mentioned a couple of familiar names, amused by her awed response.

'They're just people, like you and me.'

'Like you, perhaps.' They had reached the steps. Nicola followed him up. On the deck, she said tentatively, 'Have you thought any more about moving back out here permanently?'

'Not yet,' he admitted. 'I've barely had chance!' He turned his head to look at her, his expression hard to define with any accuracy. 'Are you pushing me for a decision?'

Bearing in mind what he said earlier about confidence, there was only one answer to that. 'Yes.'

His laugh was low. 'I'll have somebody clean the place up.'

'I could do that,' she offered eagerly. 'I'd like to!'

'You can supervise.' He leaned against the rail, drawing her to him to hold her between his thighs while he kissed the end of her nose. 'You're going to need a car, for starters. An open-top, I think.'

Her senses were drowning. She said weakly, 'Always assuming I hold a valid licence, of course.'

'You don't drive?'

'I meant valid over here.'

'No reason why it shouldn't be.' He ran his finger lightly down her spine to take a hip in each hand and gently rotate her pelvis. 'You feel good!'

'I feel anything but,' she moaned, eyes closed to the exquisite sensation. 'Ross, we're on public view!'

'So let's go inside,' he suggested on a rougher note.

They didn't make it as far as the bedroom this time. Nicola didn't care. The thick, soft carpet was more than adequate support. If she gave him nothing else, she could give him this, she told herself as they came together, then all thought faded into the white-hot heat of consummation.

It was later, on the way back, that he dropped the bombshell.'

'We're going to be giving a party,' he said. 'Next week. You won't have to worry about planning it,' he added, turning his head and catching her expression. 'The caterers will take care of the whole thing.'

'It wasn't the planning I was thinking about,' Nicola confessed. 'I could cope with that.'

Dark brows lifted. 'For two hundred?'

The sinking of her heart was no imaginary sensation. 'Two hundred?'

'It's time you met some people,' he stated unequivocally. 'And they you, if it comes to that.'

'*Some* people, perhaps,' she rallied. 'Not the whole goddam city!'

His grin almost melted her. 'You're even leaning to swear like an American.'

'With just cause.' She was silent for a moment, trying to rationalise her emotions. 'Why not wait till we move out to the beach, and then make it a smaller affair?' she asked at length.

'Because it's better this way. Let them all get a good look at you, then we can forget it.' He waited for some reply, glancing her way when she failed to make one. 'As I said before, they're only people.'

'People who knew you when Arlene was alive,' she returned huskily. 'I'm not sure I can take the comparison.'

He gave an impatient sigh. 'You're two totally different types. Anyway, it's settled. Invitations already went out.'

'I see.' She was suddenly, furiously angry. 'Then there's not much point in discussing it, is there?'

'Not a lot.' He sounded like the man she had first known, his voice coolly controlled. 'I warned you what to expect back here. If you didn't think you could handle it, you should have said so then.'

The anger died as swiftly as it had arisen. Nicola said hollowly, 'I wasn't given time to think about anything much.'

'Does that mean you regret it?'

She made an effort to pull herself together. 'No, I don't regret it. Just don't steamroller me, that's all.

His laugh was short. 'You think I make too many demands?'

'No.' She was miserably aware that they were coming close to having their first real row. 'Can we talk about something else for now? It's been too good a day to spoil.'

A pause followed her appeal; he seemed to be making some effort himself. When he spoke again, it was on a neutral note. 'You're right, let's forget it.'

The party wasn't mentioned again, but the arrangement stayed. Nicola discovered that much two days later, when the catering firm sent out a couple of frontmen to look over the premises. She would have nothing to worry about, she was assured. Every detail would be taken care of, even down to the flower arrangements. Because there was a good chance of rain at this time of year, it was decided to errect a marquee around the pool area. Watching the two of them measure up for size, she wondered drily if they were catering for two hundred or six!

By the time Ross arrived home that evening, she had persuaded herself into a frame of mind whereby she could actually talk about the coming event without wanting to stab him in the back for his lack of understanding. It was ridiculous, she conceded, to expect him to keep her under wraps just because she lacked the guts to face a few curious eyes. As an actress, she had the ability to play a part. Her performance on the night would be a measure of just how good an actress she was.

As it turned out, the evening in question was fine and dry and warm, but by then the marquee was already up, the draped satin lining and glittering chandeliers an incongruous extension to the inner regions of the house. At least they had left the pool itself outside, Nicola was glad to note from the bedroom as she prepared to meet their guests. It would be somewhere to retire to for a cooling-off period if the going got too tough.

She was wearing a long and simple sheath of blue silk, its only decoration a collar of tiny pearls set snugly about her throat. Her hair she had scooped up to the top of her head to dangle in a cascade of little curls down the back, semi-Grecian style. Make-up she kept to a deliberate minimum, but she still felt ready for the stage. Perhaps a good thing in a way, she told herself in an attempt to instil self-confidence. Waiting in the wings was always the most nerve-racking part of any production. Once out there on the boards, she would find her character.

Ross came out from the bathroom, pursing his lips into a soundless little whistle as he looked at her.

'Like a million dollars!' he said.

Her smile was only slightly forced. 'A bit different from the bedraggled creature you picked up that night in Venezuela.'

'Very.' He turned to a mirror to adjust his tie. 'Not

only in appearance, either.'

'Compliment or complaint?' she queried lightly.

'Just an observation. Circumstances govern behaviour.'

'That's the director in you coming out.' She finished screwing in the small pearl ear-rings, taking a last fleeting glance in the cheval-glass before firmly relegating her appearance to the back of her mind. 'What time do you think they'll start arriving?'

'Any minute, I'd say.' Ross left the tie alone, turning back to face her. 'How does this look?'

Magnificent, she wanted to say, only she wouldn't have been referring to the tie. In the slim-cut black trousers and white tuxedo, Ross was a king among men. He had seemed a little offhand these past couple of days, enough so to make her hesitant in going to him now. 'I'm sure you've tied one often enough to know it's fine,' was all she allowed herself. 'Do we go down now, or wait for the first arrivals?'

'Now,' Ross decided. 'I need a drink.'

He wasn't alone in that, she thought. Taken in moderation, alcohol would at least give her a boost.

The drink was not to be forthcoming for half an hour or more. They had only just reached the foot of the stairs when the doorbell chimed, heralding the first of an influx of arriving guests.

The caterers had provided a whole uniformed staff for the evening, leaving Mr and Mrs Graham free to make their own plans. There was even a butler to open the door and take wraps and so on. Standing at Ross's side while introduction after introduction was performed, Nicola could feel her smile growing stiff, her tongue freezing into an ungovernable lump. There were faces she recognised, others to which she couldn't relate the names that filled her head. Off-screen, many of the former looked less than life-size. One star in particular, a man whom she had hero-worshipped from an early age, proved to be almost bald and suffering from a bad case of halitosis. The blonde clinging to his arm was one of the most beautiful girls Nicola had ever seen, although she did little but giggle.

'Dumb as they come,' Ross muttered in cruel aside when the couple had moved on.

For herself, Nicola felt like a goldfish in a bowl. She could sense the speculation behind every glance, catch the occasional whispered comment. She wasn't what anyone had expected, from what she could gather. She wondered just what they had expected. Another sultry brunette, perhaps—a substitute for the wife Ross had lost? Couldn't they see that the last thing he needed was any reminder? He had been drawn to her because of that very difference, not just in colouring but in total personality. She might lack Arlene's stunning beauty, but she could give him something hitherto lacking from his life, and that was genuine love. It was a thought worth clinging to right now.

Sam and Velma Walker arrived around ten. Both of them short and dark and fiftyish, they looked more like brother and sister than husband and wife. Nicola liked Velma instantly, mostly because the other made no attempt to conceal her feelings.

'I must say, you're a relief!' she exclaimed. 'I don't blame Ross for keeping you away from this degenerate lot as long as he could. Good bones, wouldn't you say, Sam?'

'Sure has,' agreed her husband. 'Ever thought of doing a screen test?'

'She's not interested.' Ross was smiling, but the smile didn't reach his eyes.

'Supposing you let the girl answer for herself,' returned the older man, neither put out nor off. He lifted salt-and-pepper eyebrows to Nicola. 'How about it?'

Nicola smiled herself, and shook her head. 'I'm flattered, but Ross is quite right. Getting into films isn't an ambition of mine.'

'So what is?' he demanded.

Out of the corner of her eye, she saw Ross turn to greet a new arrival, saw a pair of white arms slide around his neck and heard a low, mocking voice purring, 'You never did waste any time, did you, darling?'

'I prefer live theatre,' she said, trying to keep her attention fixed on the Walkers. 'Not that I've done a lot of that, either.'

Sam looked interested. 'Stage school?'

'RADA,' she acknowledged.

Someone called Sam's name, waving to him through the throng of people between them. He waved back, then said succinctly, 'Get Ross to bring you down to the studios.'

'He's impressed,' murmured Velma as she moved to follow in his wake. 'Looks *and* brains—that's really something!'

She was gone before Nicola could find any answer, leaving her to turn slowly back to where Ross and the newcomer were still standing so close. In her four-inch silver kid heels, the woman was almost as tall as he was, her superb body wrapped in shimmering lamé. She wore diamonds at her throat and on both wrists, the inset emeralds almost exactly matching her wide-set eyes. Hair the colour of rich dark burgundy was layered about her arresting face. Nicola knew who she was, of course. There could be few people who wouldn't recognise Paula Reddington. From the length of time she had been a star of the silver screen, she had to be in her late thirties, yet she looked no more than twenty-eight. Not a single line marred the smooth perfection of her features.

'So introduce me to your wife, darling!' she said now, looking over Ross's shoulder to where Nicola stood waiting. Her laugh was low and husky, tinged with malice. 'You mustn't neglect your bride.'

Grey eyes met blue as he turned, the former devoid of expression. Nicola seized the initiative, switching on a smile of her own. 'Paula Reddington hardly needs an introduction,' she said. 'Anyone would know who you were.'

Finely drawn eyebrows lifted a fraction. 'You're a fan of mine?'

'My mother was for years.' It was a downright lie, but she was in no mood to care. Childish or not, the shaft had struck home. She could tell from the sudden intake of breath, the leap of anger in the green eyes.

'How nice,' she said. 'Ross, darling,' putting a hand on his sleeve, 'I'm gasping for a drink!' Without looking at Nicola, she added lightly, 'You don't mind if I borrow him for a few minutes? Only Ross can mix a Martini the way I like it.'

'He's a free agent,' Nicola retorted, conscious of the faint compression about his mouth. 'Borrow away.'

Left alone, she abandoned any further late-comers to their own devices and forced herself to move in among the throng of people. Over the following hour or so she was put through what amounted to a third degree, some of it subtle, some of it not so. She fended off the more intrusive questions with a smile and a vague answer. Where and how she and Ross had met was their business, no one else's.

She kept catching glimpses of him through the crowd—always, it seemed, with Paula Reddington in close proximity. That there had been something between the two of them in the past, she was fairly sure, but it was the here and now that concerned her most. Paula was of Ross's world; she talked the same language. Perhaps, she thought dully, he was already beginning to realise the mistake he had made in marrying someone from outside it.

She had to get out of here, if only for a few minutes, she told herself at that point. Both body and mind craved a breath of unconditioned air.

It was pleasantly warm outside. The noise from within lost its edge as she moved around the pool to the outer curve of the terrace and the magnificent view. Ross hadn't mentioned the move out to the beach house again; she could only hope that he still had it in mind. She wanted badly to leave this place. There were no photographs of Arlene around that she had seen, but her presence was everywhere. This house was her creation, the other was Ross's own. Despite the evidence left there, the atmosphere had been quite different.

'Why don't you join me?' asked a voice from somewhere behind and below her, and she turned with a start, her back against the rail as she looked at the still, clear water. The floodlight dimmers were in operation, creating shadows across the surface. It took her moment to pick out the head bobbing a few feet from the nearside, another to recognise the young man she vaguely recalled being introduced as the male lead in *The Spoilers*, although she had taken little real note of his blond good looks at the time.

'The water's fine,' he added. 'Perfect night temperature. You'll not catch cold.'

Without moving, she said, 'I gather you're not wearing anything yourself?'

'Right on.' White teeth flashed. 'Shocked?'

'No. Just not about to play follow-my-leader.'

'I give it another half an hour at the most before somebody else gets the same idea. Renata's bored. That means trouble.' He had come to the edge, hooking an arm over the rim to hoist himself up a little. Darkened by moisture, the blond hair was sleek to his head. He was well built, Nicola noted, his shoulders and arms muscular without being heavy.

Honesty was the only way out of her dilemma. 'I'm afraid,' she said, 'I can't quite remember your name. There were so many people . . .'

His grin was attractive. 'I haven't made the big-time yet. It's Keir Lawson.'

'Is that your real name?'

'No,' he admitted. 'That's Bobby Bailey.'

'Doesn't have the same box-office appeal,' she agreed. 'I'll stick to Keir. You arrived with your co-star, didn't you?'

'Renata Morant. She's the one I was talking about.'

Nicola regared him with her head tilted. 'You didn't sound terribly impressed.'

'I'm not. If you want the truth, she's a bitch. The only reason we came together tonight was because it's expected. She can't stand me, either.'

'Doesn't it affect your performance together at all?' Nicola asked, and the grin came again.

'I just imagine I'm with someone else during the love scenes. It's a love-hate relationship, anyway. We sure don't have to act the hate!' His head was tilted back, showing the clean line of his throat. 'That's enough about me. How come Ross found you first?

She kept her tone light. 'We met in Venezuela.'

'Was that where he disappeared to? Nobody knew. Couldn't believe my luck when I heard he was going to direct *The Spoilers.*'

'Is this your first film?' she asked.

Keir nodded. 'I had the luck to be in the right place at the right time when they were casting. If it doesn't make it, it's back to the sidelines again. Second chances don't come easy.'

'It will make it,' she assured him, smiling. 'One look at you and the female population will be clamouring for more!'

Keir laughed. 'I like it!' Pale sparkling blue in colour, his eyes rested on her face. 'You know,' he added on a softer note, 'it's a real treat to be with a female who isn't bitching about everything and everyone. You're out of another mould, Nicola. I could easily fall in love with you.'

She laughed, taking him no more seriously than she was sure he meant to be taken. 'I can bitch with the best, given the incentive.'

'And Ross doesn't provide it?'

Her throat went a little tight. 'Not in any measure.'

'Guess he knows when he's well off.' There was a pause, another change of tone. 'Are you sure you won't come on in?'

She shook her head. 'I have to get back. I only slipped out for a moment.'

'Escaped, you mean.' The blond hair was springing back to life as it shed moisture. 'These affairs are all alike—same faces, some old gossip. I used to see Hollywood as some kind of magic kingdom where dreams could come true. It might have been once, only not any more. That lot in there would stab each other in the back and smile while they were doing it!'

'Disillusionment at such an early age?' Nicola kept her tone deliberately light. 'If it's really that bad, you could always give it up and go back to being what you were before.'

'No, thanks.' Keir was grinning, unabashed by the gentle dig. 'I'll suffer for my art.'

The muted sound of voices and music grew suddenly louder as the sliding doors through which Nicola herself had emerged were opened to emit a laughing group. Renata Morant was at their head, long dark hair swinging abut her bare shoulders.

'Last one in's a dummy!' she shouted, stripping off the strapless dress as she made for the pool, and kicking the dress carelessly to one side, along with her stiletto-heeled sandals. She was naked beneath, except for a pair of flimsy Tanga-style briefs, her body golden in the soft light.

The others followed her, some stripping down as she had done, one or two not bothering to remove anything at all. The splashes as they hit the water were accompanied by screams and shouts, the noise deafening. Renata had to be the youngest among them, Nicola realised, too stunned to move as she watched the party cavort, but she was certainly the ringleader.

Keir was making his way around the edge of the pool to where he had left his clothing when his co-star spotted him, her whole face lit by sudden malice as she called attention to his presence. Before he could heave himself from the water he was dragged into their midst, with Renata teasing him, taunting him, calling his masculinity into question with a turn of phrase Nicola could scarcely credit.

Goaded beyond restraint, he went for her, the two of them disappearing below the surface in a welter of arms and legs.

The noise must have penetrated through into the house itself, because people were coming out to see what was going on, some laughing at the spectacle, others patently disdainful of the riff-raff in their midst, a few revealing the same disgust Nicola was feeling. When Ross appeared the way was cleared for him right to the pool edge.

Without apparently raising his voice more than a fraction, because Nicola could barely hear it from where she stood, he ordered everybody out of the water. He was furious; she could tell that from the taut line of his jaw. And rightly so. This surely wasn't his kind of scene.

At first it seemed no one was going to take any heed, then slowly the noise began to subside, the partakers becoming sheepishly aware of what fools they were all making of themselves. Only Renata retained her initial exuberance, kicking up a clean pair of heels as she went after Keir who was swimming for the far side of the pool. He reached it ahead of her, drawing himself hastily from the water to snatch up his clothing from the lounger where he had left it, and retire to a darker corner.

Two of the hired staff appeared, arms full of towels. Sobered by now, the people in the pool began getting out, wrapping themselves in the towels and vanishing indoors. Renata was the last. Quite unashamed of her nudity, she pulled herself up the ladder almost at Ross's feet.

'It was just a bit of fun,' she said with a look that defied him to make anything of it. 'It livened the party up, anyway!'

'And some,' he agreed, disarming her far more effectively than any amount of invective. The towel he took from one of the hired staff was large enough to swamp the girl's slender figure. 'Use one of the bedrooms, if you can find one empty. Someone will bring you your things.'

With the fun over, the rest of the party began to filter back indoors in Renata's wake. Ross stayed where he was, gazing across the pool to where Nicola still stood against the balustrade.

'Enjoying yourself?' he asked.

'Not so as you'd notice,' she said, borrowing his tone. 'I just happened to be out here. And, to set the record quite straight, Keir Lawson was already in the water before they came out.'

'Talking to you?'

'Yes.' She pressed herself away from the rail. 'It's time we went back inside.'

'Stay where you are,' he shot at her. 'I'll come over there.'

She watched him coming—tall, lean, and at this moment an utter stranger to her. She had never seen him in such narrow-eyed anger before. This wasn't the man she loved; this was someone else.

'Before you say anything,' she stated when he reached her, 'you're going to listen. I'm not taking any blame for something that had nothing to do with me—nor should Keir, if it comes to that. He didn't instigate what happened, Renata did.'

'You mean, she stripped him?'

Nicola bit her lip. 'If you're going to take that attitude, there's not much point in talking about it at all.'

Ross had stopped a couple of feet away, hands thrust into trouser pockets. 'I don't want my wife mixed up with that crowd.'

'You invited them,' she pointed out. 'From what Keir tells me, Renata Morant is trouble wherever she is. Why complain because she lives up to her reputation?'

'Morant's a detail. Lawson has an eye to the main chance.'

'Meaning he might believe I could help him further his career?' Her voice was brittle. 'What influence am I likely to have?'

'Who knows? You're moving in the right circles.'

The wall at her back was no more unyielding than the one facing her. She said tightly, 'No, I'm not. This whole event was in your interests, Ross, not mine. If it's the truth you're after, I've hated almost every minute!'

Dark brows lifted sardonically. 'Maybe I under-estimated your ability to act a part.'

'Maybe you did. Maybe I did.' Her nails were digging into her palms, her whole body tense. 'This isn't my world. I'm not sure it ever could be. But I'll do my best to fit in, if that's what you want. Sometimes,' she added on a bitter note, 'I don't think you know what you *do* want!'

There was a pause before he answered that one. When he did speak, it was with a certain wry inflection. 'You could have a point. Sam Walker wanted to talk to you. Let's go and find him.'

Nicola took the hand he stretched out to her, aware that his smile was merely a cover for emotions he wasn't about to reveal. She felt churned up herself, reluctant to face the avid curiosity of those inside. Their relationship was altering, and not for the better. Somehow she had to stop the slide before it gathered too much momentum. Putting Paula Reddington to the back of her mind was the first step.

A small crowd was gathered about the great man. Sam greeted her with what she was to learn was a typical lack of finesse.

'About time you tore yourself away from those young vagabonds and paid some attention to those who matter!'

There were grins from those about them. Nicola allowed herself a smile of her own. 'I'll bear it in mind, Mr Walker.'

Shrewd eyes acquired a sudden twinkle. 'Call me Sam,' he invited. 'That accent of yours cuts like glass.'

'I'll try to temper it.' She was conscious of Ross moving away again. Later, there would be time to sort out the whole silly business, for now, she had to school herself to forget it. 'After all,' she added, 'when in Rome . . .'

'US of A will do.' He was studying her with intent. When he spoke again, it was as if to the company in general. 'See what I mean?'

It was one of the other men who answered him, his voice as thoughtful as Sam's. 'You're right, she's spot-on for the part. If she can act into the bargain, we might be in busines.'

'I can act,' declared Nicola with a coolness she was far from feeling, 'but I'm no bargain. Would it be too much to ask what you're talking about?'

'Would you listen to that!' Sam sounded jubilant. He saw Nicola's face, and added kindly, 'We've got a property that's already cast, except for the female lead.

It's about this Englishwoman who comes out here to
live around the beginning of the century. Lot more to it
than that, of course, but you can read the script to find
out.' He turned his attention back to the other speaker.
'How soon can you set up a test?'

The man shrugged. 'Tomorrow.'

'I hate to put a spanner in any works,' Nicola broke in
before Sam could answer, 'only you seem to have
forgotten one minor point.'

All eyes became fixed on her, Sam's mildly curious.
'What's that?'

She took a deep breath, unable to quite believe that
this was really happening to her. 'You didn't ask me if I
were willing to consider the part.'

The silence which greeted that statement could be
felt. Nicola wanted suddenly to giggle at the blank
astonishment on all faces. Sam was the first to break the
pause.

'You're in no position to start dictating terms yet.'

'I am,' she returned, 'if it's you who wants me, rather
than the other way round. As it happens, I'm not
attempting to dictate anything. I'm grateful for the
thought, of course, but I'm not interested in taking it
up, thank you.'

'You've got to be mad!' exclaimed one of the women
on a note of conviction. 'You're being offered the
chance of a part any actress in town would give their
right arm for!'

'A one-armed heroine would certainly be different!'
Nicola let her smile fade when nobody laughed. 'Look,
I'm sorry,' she added unhappily. 'I'm not trying to be
difficult, or act the prima donna. I don't have any
experience to offer. I only left drama school six months
ago. Since then, I've played one small part in a play that
folded after a couple of weeks.' She attempted another
laugh, aware of the total lack of understanding in those
listening to what she said. 'I'd probably fail the screen

test, in any case!'

'We won't know that till we see you.' Sam was doing his best to show patience. 'Tomorrow . . .'

'No!' She was desperate to get the message across. 'Please will you listen? I don't *want* the part.'

'I don't believe that.' Sam Walker was obviously not a man accustomed to having his plans thwarted. Only an inch or so taller than she was, he nevertheless seemed to tower over her as he seized her elbow in a firm grasp. 'We're going to talk about this, just the two of us.'

Nicola went with him. Short of cutting from the room, there seemed no reasonable alternative. He led the way to a relatively quiet corner, behind a huge potted palm, waving her into a seat and taking one himself that effectively cut off any line of escape on her part.

'Now,' he said purposefully, 'supposing you tell me what's really behind this.'

Nicola lifted her shoulders in a helpless little movement. 'I didn't come here to break into films.'

'So what's that got to do with anything? Trying to tell me you've lost interest in acting altogether?'

'No,' she said, not caring to elaborate on her inner feelings. 'At least, not in the long term.'

'Long term, short term, what the hell is that supposed to mean?' The patience was rapidly wearing thin. 'If Ross is the problem, say so and I'll talk to him.'

She took a grip on herself, meeting the studio head's eyes without a flicker. 'It doesn't have anything to do with Ross. I don't have any desire at all to work in films. I realise that must be difficult for you people to understand, only that's the way it is. I'm . . . sorry. Truly.'

For a long moment, he seemed about to argue further, then he sighed and shook his head. 'You're right, I don't understand. There are thousands of unknowns out there who'd jump at the chance you've been offered.'

'Then surely it shouldn't be too difficult to find one just as suited to the part as you appear to believe I would have been.'

'Luck like that doesn't strike twice,' he growled. 'We'll have to settle for one of the short-list.' He made a final appeal. 'If you just took the screen test . . .'

'It would be a waste of time.' She hesitated before adding tentatively, 'I'd like to think of you as a friend, Sam. You *and* Velma. I know so few people in LA.'

'Sure you can.' He leaned over and patted her hand in fatherly fashion, driving his disappointment under where it didn't show so much. 'You and Ross should come over and spend Christmas with us. The kids will be home.'

Christmas was less than two weeks away, Nicola realised in shock. The Californian climate was apt to make one forget dates. 'It sounds lovely,' she said. 'Ask Ross, will you? He's the one who makes the plans.'

'Most American women wouldn't let him,' came the dry response. 'Ask Velma who runs our family.

'But not the studio,' Nicola returned slyly, and saw him smile.

'That's another ball game.' There was a pause and a change of tone. 'Ross tells me you're the one who talked him into coming back home. If that's true, we owe you a lot. Directors of his calibre are few and far between.'

'I like to think I helped.' She felt warmed by the knowledge that Ross himself had shown recognition. 'But he'd have come back eventually, whatever.'

'Maybe.' He heaved himself to his feet, looking at her with narrowed appraisal. 'Don't think I gave up yet. I didn't get where I am by taking no for an answer.'

He was gone before she could form any further denial. Thinking about it, Nicola was bound to admit that the idea excited her a little. Few people could fail to

be stirred by such an offer. She wondered whether
Ross had known what Sam wanted to talk about, and
what his reactions might be. Not that it made any
difference. Just playing the part of his wife was
enough to be going on with!

CHAPTER SEVEN

IT WAS almost three o'clock when the last guests departed. Seeing Paula Reddington off the premises with Ross at *her* side gave Nicola a fleeting satisfaction.

She was relieved that Sam made no further reference to the screen test, yet at the same time had to confess to a certain regret. Had she not been married to Ross, her response might very well have been different. On the other hand, prompted the voice of reason, had she not been married to Ross, it was most unlikely that she would ever have come to Los Angeles at all, much less found herself in the company of such an eminent personage as Sam Walker.

Ross himself was quiet as they prepared for bed. Only when he finally slid between the sheets at her side, and reached for her, did Nicola feel the tension in her relax.

'I was rough on you tonight,' he said, low-toned. 'I needed an outlet, and you bore the brunt.'

An outlet for what? came the thought. She said softly, 'It isn't important, Ross. None of those people are important.'

His movement was abrupt. 'They are to me.'

'I meant on a personal not a professional basis. How many could you count on in a real crisis?'

'A couple, maybe,' he admitted after a moment. 'Three, at a pinch.'

Was one of them Paula? Nicola wondered. 'There you are, then,' she said.

He put his lips to her throat. 'And here *you* are. My level-headed Saxon bride!'

There may have been just a hint of irony in the comment, but she chose to ignore it. Her response to his kisses was, as always, without restraint, blotting out the last lingering memory of that other darkly beautiful face. She loved this man too much to let their differences come between them, she thought fiercely. Marriage wasn't all a bed of roses; it took adjustment from both sides. They would work things out.

She awoke late to find herself alone in the bed. Mr King had gone out over an hour ago, the housekeeper told her when she got downstairs. He hadn't said where he was going, nor how long he might be. Basking in the warm, Sunday sunshine out by the pool, Nicola felt last night's doubts come seeping back. Their lovemaking might be everything it needed to be for her, but was it for Ross? Paula Reddington wasn't the kind to worry about a minor inconvenience like a wife.

It was gone one-thirty when she heard the car coming up the drive. She stayed where she was, a pair of dark glasses covering her eyes. Ross was wearing casual trousers and a light sweater when he appeared. Nicola steeled herself to accept the light kiss he dropped on the top of her head.

'Hungry?' she asked.

'I ate at the club,' he said. 'Didn't Mrs Graham tell you?'

Relief was the uppermost emotion. 'No, she didn't. What club?'

'Golf. It's been an age since I last played. Hasn't done my game any good.' He was making for the poolside bar as he spoke. 'I'm for a long cold drink. Want one?'

'Nothing alcoholic,' she said. 'I had enough last night.'

'Not as much as some.' There was a pause, an alteration in tone. 'I partnered Sam this morning. He seems to think I might be stopping you doing a test.'

'I didn't tell him that,' she denied.

'You must have implied it.' He came over to hand her a glass, studying her narrowly. 'Do you want to do it?'

She closed her mind against the small, dissenting voice. 'No, of course not. I'm no film actress.'

'It's a different technique from live theatre,' he agreed. 'Not so much acting as the ability to project a personality.'

'Isn't that much the same thing?'

'No, it isn't. The best film actors are those capable of being themselves in front of the camera. That's not as easy as it might seem. The reason Sam thinks you might make the perfect Catherine is because you look and sound like his concept of her.' Ross dropped to a seat on the lounger at her side, taking a long pull at the glass in his hand before adding, 'The Same Sky is his pet project. He thinks the climate is right for a return to the good old-fashioned love story. Did you read the book? It's done surprisingly well out here.'

'Mary Gillen, isn't it? Yes, I've read it.' Nicola was unable to deny the stirring of interest. The book had been good. It had made her laugh, it had made her shed a tear to two, it had created instant empathy with the heroine, Catherine Devonshire, who had sacrificed a whole way of life for love of a man with whom she had almost nothing in common. A peach of a part by any standards. She said slowly, 'Do you think the climate is right?'

Ross shrugged. 'Could be. Then again, maybe not. If public tastes were predictable, we'd all be billionaires!' He rolled his head to glance at her, his smile somehow lacking in spontaneity. 'This has to be the first time Sam has ever had an offer refused.'

Nicola kept her tone light. 'There has to be a first time for everything.'

'So they say. I understand we're invited over for Christmas. An honour I've certainly never been accorded before.'

'Perhaps he didn't think Arlene would have enjoyed their type of Christmas,' she said.

'He could have been right. We spent our last one in Vegas.'

It was a shock to realise that little more than a year ago Arlene had still been alive. From the sudden tension in his jawline, Ross was thinking much the same thing. She said huskily, 'When were you thinking of making the move out to the beach, Ross?'

He was lying back again, eyes closed against the sun's glare. 'You'll be doing most of the organising. It's up to you.'

'But you want to go?' she insisted.

'Yes, I want to go. You've got the Porsche, and your licence is good for a few months, so there's nothing to stop you running out there to keep an eye on things. Just let me know when you're ready.'

Who do I get in to refurbish the place? she was about to ask, then stopped herself. Handle it, he was saying in effect, so handle it she would. It would be something to do, something to enjoy—something to take her mind off the doubts still lurking. Loving a man was one thing, knowing his inner self quite another. There was still so much about Ross that she didn't understand, couldn't get close to.

His attitude just now when he had spoken about the part Sam was offering her was difficult to define: not exactly pressing her to have a go, yet not discouraging her, either. Perhaps she was being oversensitive in thinking he wouldn't want her involved in film-making. Not that it made any real difference either way, because she had no intention of doing anything about it. Sam would have to find someone else to play his precious Catherine.

It took a couple of weeks to get the beach house ready

for full-time occupation again. With a free hand and an open cheque book, Nicola decided on a change of décor while she was at it, choosing pastel shades of blue and lemon, with off-white covers for chairs and sofas, and filmy sheers to replace the heavy satins at the downstairs windows.

The main bedroom she refurbished completely, feeling no compunction over consigning the dark and bulking furnishings to the basement, replacing them with stripped pine and brass. The window shutters were painted gloss white, bringing light into the rooms even when they were closed against the occasional seasonal storm.

Ross registered neither approval nor disapproval of the changes. Sometimes Nicola wondered if he even noticed what she was doing to the place. They were on schedule with the studio shoot, she gathered, and due to depart north to San Francisco right after the Christmas break. So far he had said nothing about taking her with them, yet the thought of staying here in Los Angeles without him was hardly enticing. It was up to her to make it clear that she both expected and wanted to go, she supposed, only the opening somehow never arose.

Mrs Graham had not mentioned the impending move, although the Beverley Hills house was already on the market. That their services would hardly be required out at the beach went without saying; the house itself was small enough to be adequately serviced by a daily domestic. Nicola could only conclude that Ross intended to make up for the lack of notice with a financial settlement of some kind when the time came. Money was no object in this neck of the woods. Not while one's services were still in demand, at any rate.

The fact that she herself would have preferred Ross to be rather less involved in his job was neither here nor there. He was back where he belonged. In part, she could take credit for that. Had she not happened along that fateful night, he might well still be stagnating in that Venezuelan backwater. The part of her that wished they both were she kept well hidden. This was her life now, as much as his. She had to make the best she could of it, for both their sakes.

Making the best of it involved, among other things, accepting at least a few of the invitations which came pouring in. Gradually, she acquired a surface sang-froid. It was inevitable that they should run into Paula Reddington from time to time, but even she was not allowed to penetrate the veneer. If this marriage was to stand any chance of succes, trust was an essential factor.

With the beach house finally ready for occupation, it was simply a case of arranging the actual transfer, yet she hesitated to broach the subject. The first intimation she had of any move on Ross's part was via Mrs Graham herself one morning shortly after he had left for the studio.

Bringing coffee out to the terrace, the woman showed no immediate inclination to depart, her well groomed features set in lines of contempt.

'I knew you'd be trouble the minute I set eyes on you,' she declared. 'Judd and I have given three years of our lives to looking after this place, and small thanks we get for it! You did it, didn't you? You persuaded him to get out.'

'He never liked it here,' Nicola began in self-defence, the caught herself up as she realised she owed no explanations. 'I'm sure you were very well paid for all you've done,' she said instead, 'and I doubt if you'll have much difficulty in finding another position.'

'Oh, that's going to be no problem. We can pick and choose.' The contempt hadn't lessened. 'It doesn't alter the fact that you've made it necessary. We were settled here.'

There was no way, Nicola thought, that she was going to be made to feel totally responsible for their loss. It was hers and Ross's lives that had to matter most. 'I'm not surprised,' she said coolly. 'For almost a year you had it to yourselves. Living off the fat of the land, I think it's called. Anyway, it's done, so there's not much point in talking about it, is there?'

'Point enough.' The older woman's mouth was a thin tight line, her eyes agate hard. 'Don't imagine you're going to make him forget his wife. She was more woman than you'll ever be! You're nothing more than a cheap little pick-up. He'll throw you out with the rest of the garbage when he's had everything you've got to offer—and that shouldn't take long.'

'I think you've said enough.' Nicola was fighting to retain the same cool detachment. 'Please leave.'

'We're doing that today. So make the most of the coffee, it's the last you'll get made for you.'

Nicola clenched her teeth against the sharp reply as the other moved off. What was the use? The things Mrs Graham had said hurt, and would go on hurting for a long time, but she couldn't allow it to show. If Ross had been here, this conversation would never have taken place. Why leave her to bear the brunt?

The Grahams left around noon. With the house entirely to herself for the very first time, Nicola made a foray into the kitchen area. The huge refrigerator was well stocked, the freezer equally so. Food enough to last a family of six several weeks, she calculated. Mrs Graham was good at her job; she couldn't fault her on that. All the same, they must have lived like kings themselves during the months Ross had been away!

Always before she had put off exploring that part of the house shared by Ross and his first wife. With departure now assured, the curiosity could no longer be stilled. As with the suite they now occupied, there was both sitting-room and bedroom, the two of them luxuriously—if a little too ornately for her own taste—equipped. The wardrobes were empty, all personal items removed. Nicola wondered if Ross himself had instigated the clearing out, or if Mrs Graham had taken it on herself to wipe away the traces. Either way, Arlene had gone for good. That was how it was going to stay, she told herself resolutely. From now on, she was the only Mrs King.

She was contemplating a swim when Ross arrived home unexpectedly at three.

'The gates were open,' he said. 'Somebody call?'

'The Grahams left,' Nicola told him. 'I forgot to push the button after them.'

'You shouldn't. There's no knowing who might walk on in.' He registered what she had actually said with a sudden frown. 'Left?'

She looked at him swiftly. 'You didn't know they were going today?'

'If I had, I wouldn't be asking,' he said without particular inflection. 'They were supposed to stay another week.'

'We'll manage.' She added casually. 'You're early. Did something go wrong?'

'No, right for once, Every take a winner!' He slung his jacket over a chair back, smiling now. 'If those two can keep their differences out of it, we'll be in with a chance.'

Nicola didn't bother asking which two. Not only was it obvious, but she was still reluctant to show any interest at all in Keir Lawson's progress. 'Did you want a drink?' she asked instead.

'I'll get it,' she said. 'How about you?'

She shook her head. 'Later, perhaps. I was just going in for a swim.'

She took a header into the pool, swimming the full length underwater, to surface gasping a little because she was so out of practice. From the rim where she rested, she could see straight across to the far canyon wall, catch the glint of sunlight on glass from a semi-concealed dwelling. The scent of pine wafted on the air. She hoped Ross wasn't planning on going anywhere tonight. A quiet evening at home on their own was all she wanted right now.

Behind her there was a splash. She didn't turn her head, feeling the ripples created by his passage pushing gently against her back. Then he was there behind her, turning her into his arms, the glint in his eyes an echo of the excitement coursing through her body. He was naked, she realised, as her body cleaved to him. She made a small sound of protest when he unfastened the clip of her bikini top and drew the shielding material from between them.

'Supposing someone has binoculars on us from over there!'

'Then they're going to strike lucky,' he said.

Making love in the water was a whole new experience. It gave, Nicola decided, a quite different concept to the term 'kiss of life'. They didn't bother to dress again afterwards. It scarcely seemed worth it. Relaxing beside her on a lounger, Ross gave a sigh of contentment.

'It's worth doing without help in the house for this amount of freedom. I should have thought of it before.'

'When do we move out to the beach?' Nicola asked, seizing her chance. 'The house is all ready.'

'It doesn't matter to me,' he said. 'There's little enough, apart from personal items, I want to take with us. You name the day.'

'Friday, then.' She waited a moment before adding, 'Have you found a buyer yet?'

'Nothing concrete.' He sounded unconcerned. 'It might take a while. Don't worry about it.'

She wasn't worrying about anything, Nicola thought happily. At this precise moment, she had it all!

The move was accomplished with little fuss. For Nicola, it was a whole new beginning. She felt at home here in the house in which she herself had wrought such changes. She revelled in cooking for Ross, even in keeping the place spick and span. His suggestion that they get someone in to do the latter, at least, was met with disdain. She could manage, she said. She *wanted* to do it. Shrugging philosophically, he let her have her way. She would soon tire of the novelty, he declared.

The approach of Christmas was the only cloud on her immediate horizon. With no money of her own, how was she going to buy Ross a present? she wondered. Her signature was good in every downtown store, it was true, but she could hardly charge it to his own account. Short of finding a temporary—and illegal—job, she had no way of making any money. In any case, Ross was unlikely to see the necessity.

Velma Walker's call came out of the blue one morning. 'Just checking on the Christmas arrangements,' she said briskly. 'You are still coming?'

'Yes, of course.' Nicola was at once apologetic. 'I should have written.'

'No cause.' The other woman sounded unconcerned. 'We don't go in for formality very much. As I said, just a final head count for the table. Hope you're not allergic to either kids or animals. We've a selection of both!'

Nicola laughed. 'Not that I know of. We're both looking forward to it.'

'You, maybe; Ross, I'm not too sure of. Are you a churchgoer?'

'I like to go at Christmas,' Nicola admitted. 'I don't know about Ross.'

'It won't hurt him to sacrifice an hour. Half after nine then, so we can all travel down together.'

Nicola was aware of a sudden loneliness after Velma had rung off. It would be at least another five or six hours before Ross got back, maybe even more if he decided to stay in town for dinner as he had done the night before. Discussing technicalities with production staff, he had said by way of excuse when he'd telephoned through to warn her.

When the call came at six, she was half waiting for it. Ross sounded as if his mind were on other things.

'We're running over,' he said. 'Call a cab and meet me at L'Orangerie at nine.'

He had rung off before she could answer, leaving her to replace the receiver with decidedly mixed feelings. Was it to be dinner for just the two of them, or was she to find herself part of a crowd where the whole conversation would be above her head? That had happened once to her already; she wasn't sure she could take it again. Not that she had much choice, she acknowledged, short of phoning back to question the arrangement, and Ross would hardly appreciate being called off set in order to put her mind at rest.

She chose a pyjama suit in burgundy shot-silk as a compromise between formal and informal evening wear, teaming with it the single strand of pearls that had been the only possession of any real monetary value left by her mother. Where they had come from originally, Nicola had no idea. She liked to believe they could have been a present from her father, whoever he was. Her hair she left shining loose to her shoulders, the way Ross liked it best. There would be enough sophisticates at L'Orangerie tonight without her attempting to emulate them. She could conjure no particular thrill at the thought of dining out at one of Los Angeles' most star-studded restaurants. Who one was with counted for more than whom one might see. As Ross himself had said, they were only people—some of them not even very nice people.

The valet who came to open the cab door for her when she arrived outside the restaurant not only knew who she was but had cash in hand, ready to pay the driver on her behalf.

'Mr King rang to say he might be a little late,' the man told her smoothly. 'The *maître d'* will take care of you, ma'am.'

Had she had enough ready cash on her, Nicola would have preferred to get back in the cab and ride around for fifteen minutes rather than face a lone entry. Under the circumstances, she had little recourse but to smile and assume an air of philosophical acceptance, as if the matter were no more than a minor annoyance. Ross had no right to do this to her, she fumed underneath. Didn't he even care enough to be here when he promised?

The *maître d'hôtel* was all smiles the moment she mentioned her name. Mr King would be here shortly, he assured her. In the meantime, perhaps she would like a cocktail at the bar?

The latter was crowded, but he found her a seat close by one of the window embrasures, overlooking the classically designed courtyard. Sipping at the daiquiri almost instantly provided, Nicola tried to look as if being alone meant nothing to her, glancing around with a nonchalance she was far from feeling at the people about her. No one here she remembered meeting before—although there was certainly several familiar faces. That blond-haired Adonis over there was Tony Farrel from one of the glossy American television soaps. Better-looking off-screen than on it, she decided judiciously—at least from where she was sitting. Not a bad actor either, although the part he played in the soap opera hardly stretched him. Doing it for the money, no doubt. She couldn't blame him too much for that. The better parts would be few and far between.

'Been stood up, darling?' The drawl was soft and low, but still managed to cut like a knife. Paula Reddington had paused beside her chair, looking down at her with scarcely concealed derision in her smile.

'Ross should be shot, leaving you to stew like this!' A faint lift of a plucked eyebrow. 'It *is* Ross you're waiting for so patiently?'

'Of course.' Nicola was hard put to conceal her own inner feelings as she returned the woman's regard. 'He's coming straight from the studio.'

'Behind schedule, are they?' Paula sounded somewhat less than sympathetic. 'Well, if they will use amateurs . . .' She gave another of the false smiles. 'I do hope he isn't going to leave you sitting here all night, darling. That would be too bad of him!'

She moved on, an eye-catching figure in her clinging, royal-blue gown, followed by the male companion to whom Nicola had obviously not been deemed worthy of an introduction. Bitch! she thought caustically, and felt better for it.

The sight of Ross threading his way through the knot of people a moment or two later was a relief of such magnitude that it totally swamped the resentment she had been feeling.

'Sorry,' he proffered. 'One or two problems we had to iron out. Did you want to finish that, or shall we go straight through? I'm ravenous!'

'Then we'd better feed the brute,' she said laughingly, getting to her feet. 'You lead, I'll follow.'

Progress through to the restaurant was slowed by the number of people who hailed Ross, although he made no attempt to do more than pass the time of day. Their table was centrally placed. Nicola felt the cynosure of all eyes as she followed the *maître d'* and Ross. The realisation that the setting was only for two brought relief. She might have preferred a quieter, more intimate venue, but beggars couldn't be choosers. She was here with Ross, that was the only important factor.

He was wearing a silver-grey suit that enhanced both his breadth of shoulder and his colouring. He looked, Nicola thought, quite devastatingly male.

'I was afraid it was going to be another of those pull-it-together-over-supper kind of evenings,' she confessed when their order had been taken. 'This is nice!'

He eyed her for a moment without answering, his expression unamused. 'You find movie-talk boring?' he asked at length.

'More confusing,' she said, already regretting the observation. 'Most of the time, I've no idea what you're talking about.'

'It's my job.'

'I know.' She made an attempt to lighten the moment. 'I suppose I could always read up on the subject.'

His laugh was short. 'As easy as that!'

'No, of course not. I didn't mean it to sound . . .' She broke off, catching her lower lip between her teeth. 'Can we change the subject?'

'You opened it,' he pointed out. The lift of his shoulders signified indifference. 'So what *would* you like to talk about?'

As swiftly as that, the whole mood of the evening had altered; Nicola could feel the coolness in the air. Something was bugging him, that was obvious, but she was damned if she was going to plead with him to tell her what it was. 'I had a call from Velma Walker today,' she said.

The grey eyes took on a new expression. 'Did you now?'

'She wanted to remind me about Christmas,' Nicola ploughed on. 'As if I'd be likely to forget!'

'As if.' There was another pause, and a slight change of tone as he added, 'Was that the only reason she called?'

'What other reason could there be?'

'You tell me,' he invited. 'Sam's capable of using anyone to get his way.'

Nicola laughed. 'You make him sound totally one-track!'

'So he is. In this business, you can't afford to be anything else. And you didn't answer the question.'

She shook her head. 'The subject wasn't even mentioned.'

'So why bring it up?'

'I didn't,' she protested. 'You did.'

'Only because it was obvious that was what you were after.'

Nicola drew in a steadying breath, aware that she was coming dangerously close to losing her temper. 'How do you make that out?'

'You wouldn't have bothered mentioning Velma's call at all otherwise. There was no cause.' Ross made a sudden impatient gesture. 'If it's what you want, do it. I'm not holding you back.'

'You're not exactly bursting with enthusiasm, either,' she retorted. 'You don't believe I could do it, do you, Ross?'

He looked at her assessingly for a moment, before answering, 'You're the one who's doubtful. If you had faith in yourself, you'd say to hell with everything else.'

'The way Arlene did?' She regretted it the moment it was out, reaching an impulsive hand to cover his where it lay on the table. 'I didn't mean that.'

'It's true enough.' He sounded brusque. There was a pause, a visible effort to relax. 'It's been a hell of a day,' he added with wry inflection. 'The last thing I needed was another argument.'

The last thing she needed too, Nicola thought, but she kept her mouth shut. 'Renata?' she queried instead.

'And some! She's good, but not nearly as good as she thinks she is. The way she's acting up, this won't only be her first film, it will be her last! She held up shooting for nearly two hours this morning. She thinks Keir is getting more screen time than she is.'

'And is he?'

'No more than the storyline calls for. It's going to get worse on location.'

She wanted to ask him then if she would be going to San Francisco with them, only it didn't seem quite the time for it. They were back on even keel again for the moment. She had to content herself with that.

They were at the coffee stage when Paula and her escort dropped by.

'So you finally made it,' said the former, giving Ross the full benefit of her provocative smile. 'We thought we might join forces for a drink—didn't we, darling?' The last was said without so much as a glance in the direction of the man at her side.

'Good idea.' Ross was already on his feet, although not quite swiftly enough to forestall the waiter, who came rushing to pull up two spare chairs from another table. 'I didn't realise you were here,' he added when the newcomers were installed.

'Really?' Paula's look of surprise was over-exaggerated. 'I imagined Nicola would have told you we saw her earlier in the bar. It was rather remiss of you, darling, leaving her sitting there all alone like that.' Her laugh held a faint note of derision. 'But I guess you already had that pointed out.'

'I didn't mind waiting,' lied Nicola evenly. 'There was plenty to look at.' She smiled at the older woman's companion. 'You forgot to introduce us—darling.'

The man's lips twitched momentarily. He was younger than Paula by some four or five years, Nicola guessed, and almost too handsome. Genuine admirer, or would-be advantage-taker? she wondered. If the latter, she wished him luck.'

'Peter Jefferies,' murmured Paula with an air of uninterest. Her eyes were on Ross, sensual, wholly knowledgeable. 'Having problems?'

Nicola smiled brightly at Peter. 'Do you come here

often?'

He took the question at face value. 'Not very. It's outside my pocket.'

So Paula was paying. That knowledge afforded Nicola a certain malicious satisfaction. 'You're in films yourself?' she asked.

He shook his streaked blond head. 'I'm a tennis coach.'

'Oh?' She was taken aback for a moment, then rallied. 'A good one?'

'The best.' This time, there was no attempt to disguise the twinkle lurking in the depths of his eyes. 'I handle a lot of the big games.'

The other two were talking quietly together, lost, it seemed, to everything outside of their own immediate sphere. From the few words Nicola could catch without actually appearing to be listening in, there was nothing very private or personal in what was being said, but that didn't stop Paula from putting on the whole seduction scene, lips slightly parted, moist from the slow and tantilising passage of a tongue tip over their surface, eyes luminous, one scarlet-nailed hand resting lightly, oh, so lightly, on a grey sleeve. What Ross himself was thinking or feeling was impossible to tell, but he was making no attempt to move away. They had been lovers in the past, she was certain of it now. If Paula had anything to do with it, they would be lovers again; she was sure of that, too. Had she been as confident of Ross's love for her as she was of hers for him, she wouldn't have allowed that knowledge to bother her. As it was, she could feel the pain building inside. Jealousy was a soul-destroying emotion—one she had never had cause to experience before. She had the sudden bleak premonition that this woman was going to bring her a whole lot of pain in weeks to come.

It was later, in the car going home, that Ross said evenly, 'I was serious earlier, you know. The only person stopping you from taking that test is yourself.'

Nicola slanted a swift glance. 'You're saying you wouldn't have any objection to my getting into film work?'

'I'm saying,' he said, 'that I'd go along with it if I was convinced you could handle it. Not just the acting. The whole caboodle. You'd need to develop a whole new approach.'

'And you don't think I'm capable?'

'I don't know.' His lips twisted. 'So go ahead and find out.'

Temptation came and went. She was having enough problems making a go of marriage; taking on a new career was hardly going to help. Even if she got through the test, it wasn't to say she'd be any good in the part. And what about Ross himself? He might make all the right noises, but what did he really feel inside? Success had robbed him of one wife already. Was he really willing to risk it again—or did he simply not care deeply enough to make an issue of it?

'I don't know, either,' she said, still hoping for some insight. 'A part of me wants to say yes, I'll have a go, the other part shies away.'

'You're the only one who can decide.' He was, Nicola thought, beginning to sound bored by the whole subject. 'Only you're going to need to make up your mind pretty soon. They're due to start shooting mid-January, so the part has to be cast by the first week at the latest.'

Which gave her just two weeks to consider the options, Nicola reckoned. If she turned down this chance, she had a feeling that Sam would not be offering another. Not that an ongoing situation was bound to develop, in any case. He wanted her for Catherine purely on the strength of her visual and aural suitability, with a hope of acting ability thrown in for good measure. Should his hopes be fulfilled, it wasn't to say there would be other parts to follow. The whole film was an experiment, by all accounts. It could well turn out to be a resounding flop.

It was gone midnight when they reached the house. Somebody was holding a party along the beach, the sounds of revelry clearly audible on the night air. From the bedroom window, Nicola could see people spilling over from the rear deck on to the sands; some were in the water. A teenage party from what she could make out, although the younger element didn't hold a monopoly on skinny-dipping by any means. The Beverly Hills house had granted more privacy and peace, it was true, but she still preferred it here.

'Are you coming to bed?' asked Ross softly, already between sheets. 'Or are you planning on standing there all night?'

Turning, she was oblivious of the transparency of her nightdress as she stood silhouetted against the glass, until she heard a long, slow intake of breath. She went to join him, sliding down into his waiting arms like a pigeon coming home to roost. 'Don't let me go, Ross,' she whispered with intensity against his lips.

'I don't intend to,' he said, lowering his head to her breasts. 'We've got all night.'

It wasn't what she had meant, but she couldn't bring herself to clarify her appeal. For the moment, this had to be enough.

CHAPTER EIGHT

CHRISTMAS DAY was warm and sunny, sky and sea the same shimmering blue. The carol singing coming from the car radio seemed totally incongruous in this setting, thought Nicola on the way over to the Walkers' house. She yearned a little for snow, for red-breasted robins, for roasted chestnuts and home-made plum pudding.

'Whereas what snow there is in London will have long since turned to dirty slush, and few people have open fires to roast chestnuts over any more,' she acknowledged to Ross in an effort to dispel the nostalgia. 'Last Christmas, I was on my own in a crummy bedsit, hardly daring to switch on more than one bar of the electric fire. It's difficult to believe I'm still the same person.'

'You're not,' he said. 'The only people who stay the same are those who never do anything with their lives. You've altered since I first met you.'

She slanted a glance. 'For the better, I hope?'

His grin was reassuring. 'Depends on the viewpoint.'

Personally, Nicola reflected, she was satisfied with the one she had right now. In the lightweight beige suit and pale cream shirt, Ross was enough to warm any female heart. The pure silk tie in mingled browns and creams had been her present to him this morning. Not much on the surface, although it had cost the earth. Raising money on her mother's pearls had not been too difficult. What had surprised her was the amount offered. Making all due allowances, the string had to be worth in the region of five or six hundred pounds on the second-hand market—which gave rise to further speculation on the question of who and what her father had been. She had six months to redeem her property. After that, they would be sold.

Ross had been pleased with the tie, at any rate. He didn't own all that many. His present to her had brought a lump to her throat. It still did whenever she looked at the slim gold watch encircling her wrist. A Cartier, no less. She had never had anything this good. Unlike the clothes, the car, the thing she had bought for the beach house, this really felt as if it belonged to her. She would treasure it always, no matter what happened.

The Walkers' house was one of the grand old relics from the early twenties, not architecturally beautiful, yet somehow appealing to the eye by very virtue of that fact. The place seemed full of people and animals, the noise overwhelming. Ross was greeted with enthusiastic welcome by a whole pack of dogs in varying sizes and shapes, and fended them off with good-humoured firmness.

'About time you took this lot to obedience classes,' he said to Sam, who lifted philosophical shoulders.

'Don't tell me, tell Velma. We're about ready to go, so I won't ask you to sit down. Thought we'd all pile in together.'

In what? wondered Nicola, counting heads as the family gathered itself for the off. Apart from Velma and Sam, there was a daughter and a son, their respective partners, plus three children, ranging in ages from around seven years down to a tiny, self-contained moppet of no more than three. The latter had already attached herself to Ross with a look of out-and-out adoration that Nicola could sympathise with. She could even admit to a certain envy of the child's total lack of inhibition!

The Rolls-Royce and the stretched Mercedes waiting at the foot of the wide stone steps when they got outside, proved more than equal to the task of transporting the party. Nicola found herself seated next to the Walkers' attractive daughter Caroline, with her husband Michael and Ross occupying the two pull-downs opposite. A big, easygoing man, the former was in public relations. Within minutes, Nicola felt she had known him all her life.

The church service lasted little more than half an hour. Despite the decorated tree and beautifully arranged, almost life-size crib, Nicola could conjure no real sense of occasion. Back at the house, there was the promised brunch already prepared by a willing staff and eaten al fresco on the terrace, with the two older children having the time of their lives pedalling new tricycles around the swimming pool.

Nicola was afraid they might fall in, although with so many people on hand she supposed there wasn't all that much danger. They could probably swim like fish, anyway, she reflected. Most American children seemed able to, no matter what their age.

Ross had taken off his jacket and tie and unfastened the top button of his shirt, matching the other men, who had also relaxed. The four of them were deeply involved in a golfing discussion. Catching Nicola's eye, Caroline pulled a comically rueful face.

'Typical, isn't it? Christmas Day, and all they can talk about is birdies and eagles and slicing into the rough!'

Nicola laughed. 'I suppose it could be worse. They might be talking about work!'

'I gather you don't have much interest in the movie business? Maybe it's as well. Ross already went that route.' She caught herself up, as if only just realising what she had implied. 'Not that I'm suggesting you'd turn into another Arlene if you did take up Father's offer,' she tagged on hastily. 'You're not a bit like her.'

'I know.' They were far enough away from the others for the conversation not to be overheard. On impulse,

Nicola said, 'You knew her?'

'Who didn't?' There was an edge to the girl's voice. 'She was nothing when he met her, only she would never give him any credit for making her into a star. Without good direction, even the best actors can turn in a lousy performance, and Arlene was no Sarah B, believe me! He used to spend hours going over her lines, showing her where to lay emphasis—how to put across an emotion without even opening her mouth. I'm not saying she didn't have screen presence—she wouldn't have got through the first test without it—but it was Ross who taught her how to use it.'

He could teach her too, if he were willing, came the thought. *If.* Such a little word, so many implications.

The day went through its phases. Dinner was an absolute riot, with fancy hats and crackers and a parcel for everyone to open at the table. Nicola could hardly find the words to thank her hosts properly for the soft cashmere sweater.

'You're being so good to me,' she said. 'It's been the best Christmas I've ever spent!'

She was thankful that no one asked the obvious question. Her mother had done her best, of course, but there was nothing to beat a family circle. She felt privileged to be a part of this one, if only for a day. Watching Ross pull a cracker with one of the children, she wondered what they would be doing next year at this time. He got on surprisingly well with children; at thirty-nine, he couldn't afford to wait too long. Getting pregnant would solve her present dilemma, too—although it wasn't the best of reasons for starting a family.

Ross looked around unexpectedly and caught her eyes on him, his smile curling her insides. Later, it seemed to say. That part of their life together was everything any woman could want. So long as it lasted, came the thought, swiftly pushed to the back of her mind where it could do least damage. Some Hollywood marriages were enduring. Why not theirs? If they both worked at it.

They played a couple of games of Trivial Pursuit after the children had been put to bed. Despite the fact that the questions were geared to this side of the Atlantic, Nicola was gratified to find she could keep her end up.

'Guess none of us would have done as well on a British set,' acknowledged Michael, stacking the card trays back into the box. 'You deserve another drink for that effort. What will it be?'

Nicola asked for something long and thirst-quenching, to be rewarded with a concoction of champagne and fresh orange juice, known over here as a Mimosa. Ross was deep in conversation with Barry Walker. Michael went to join them.

From his seat on the chesterfield at Nicola's side, from where he had taken charge of his team, Sam said quietly, 'Any chance you changed your mind about the test yet?'

Her smile felt just a little stiff. 'What puzzles me,' she said on impulse, 'is why you're so insistent?'

'I don't like being turned down,' he admitted. 'Specially when I'm offering somebody a chance to *be* somebody.'

'I'm somebody now,' she said.

'Not in Hollywood you're not—unless it's Ross King's wife.' He wasn't being unkind, simply stating facts. 'I'm talking about in your own right.'

'And if I didn't come through the way you expect?'

'I'd still have the short-list to fall back on.' He was watching her face, shrewdly assessing the degree of inner conflict. 'We start shooting on the sixteenth of January. That doesn't leave too much time for a decision. All you have to say is yes.'

Nicola made a gesture of appeal. 'I just don't know, Sam.'

Wisely, he knew when not to press too far. 'So think about it. I mean seriously. I'll let you have a copy of the script. That might decide you.'

There could be no harm in taking a look, Nicola told herself.

She was quiet in the car going home. So much so that Ross was moved to remark on it.

'Just tired,' she excused herself. 'Pleasantly, though.'

'It's been a good day,' he agreed. 'I was ready for a break.'

'When will you be going to San Francisco?' she asked.

'Right after New Year,' he said. 'It's going to be a tight four weeks.'

'Do I get to come with you?'

Before he spoke, she knew what the answer was going to be. The hesitation was only too apparent. 'Location work's no picnic. We'll be working all hours. You'd be better off staying down here.'

'On my own?' Her throat felt tight.

'You'd be on your own most of the time if you came,' he said. 'I'm not going to have room for any distractions. Anyway, you don't have to be alone. There's Velma, and Caroline—they'd be glad to see you any time.'

Nicola said softly, 'I suppose I could always take that test.'

'You could.' He sounded quite dispassionate about it. 'I can set it up for this coming week, if you've decided.'

She slanted a glance at him, studying the lean features with a kind of desperation. 'You wouldn't mind?'

'It isn't up to me.' There was a trace of impatience in his tone. 'I keep telling you that. It's the chance of a lifetime for any actress—providing it's what she wants to do.'

She said slowly, 'You wouldn't be afraid I might turn into another Arlene?'

'You're not in the same mould. I've told you that before, too.'

He drew the car into the roadside, overlooking the curve of beach and the moon-silvered Pacific rollers, switching off the ignition to sit with hands resting on the wheel. Outlined against the horizon, his profile was clear-cut—achingly familiar. Nicola wanted to touch him, to reassure herself that all of this was real. Her insecurity stemmed from so many sources: the way they had met, the sheer, dreamlike quality of life in this town. If she took this chance, and achieved success, what then?

'It's time you stopped vacillating,' Ross stated. 'If you can't make up your mind, I'll make it up for you.' He turned his head to look at her, the expression in his eyes hidden in shadow. 'You're going to do that test, Nicola. If it turns out no good, then at least you'll know.'

'And if I make it?'

'Then it will give you something to occupy you while I'm away.'

'I'd be occupied when you came back, too,' she pointed out, and saw him smile a little.

'So will I. Guy likes his directors involved in post production. That takes weeks in itself. I've also got other offers to think about.' He cocked an eyebrow. 'So?'

Nicola drew a steadying breath. 'All right, I'll do it.'

Just for a moment, his jaw seemed to tauten, then he nodded, 'Good.'

He made no immediate attempt to restart the car, searching her features with a look that fired her pulses. The hand that slid behind her head to pull her to him was ungentle, his mouth equally so. Nicola felt her heart thudding against his chest, the answering heat rising from its inner core. She wanted him with an urgency that knew no limitations. It was Ross himself who did the drawing back, his mouth ironic.

'I'm past the age where making love in a car is worth the inconvenience,' he said. 'Let's get back to the house.'

The words stung. Nicola had a feeling they were meant to. What she wasn't sure of was why. But then, she acknowledged with sudden weariness, what *was* she sure of these days?

Driving through the gateway of a Hollywood film studio in a chauffeured car was an experience most people would relish, Nicola reflected, gazing through the window at the beautifully laid-out gardens fronting the site. White bungalows flanked a broad expanse of red gravel. Beyond rose the bulk of a dozen or more sound stages.

The car drew up in front of the first and most imposing of the bungalows. 'Just go right on in,' invited the chauffeur, opening the door for her. 'Mr Walker's secretary will see to things.'

Inside the sumptuously furnished reception room she was greeted by a tall, cool blonde whose looks and poise would have fitted her for a top-class model. Nicola felt intimidated until the older woman smiled.

'I'm Margot McReath,' she said. 'Mr Walker is to meet you on Stage Eight. I'm to take you across to make-up. Would you like to walk or ride? It takes a few minutes.'

'Walk, please,' Nicola returned. 'I've never been on a studio lot before.'

'You should do the Universal tour. They've more outside sets than we have.' The other cast a glance more curious than envious. 'You're a real talking point round here. The first time anybody had to be coerced into taking a screen test. Mind me asking why?'

'Self-doubt,' Nicola answered. 'Have you been with Mr Walker long?'

'Five years.' Margo could obviously take a hint. 'He's

an easy man to work for—unlike some in his postion. I like the outfit, by the way. Most first-timers overdress like crazy!'

Nicola has worn the white trousers and shirt because they were comfortable, and for no other reason. She smiled, relaxing a little. 'Thanks. You know how to say the right things.'

'All part of the job,' came the light reply. 'We'd better get across to make-up.'

A studio lot, Nicola found, was like a city in miniature. It even had its own fire department, complete with engine. There was a lake, a whole waterfront township, mock-ups of city streets; buildings that looked solid as rocks from the front and were held up by battens at the rear. Filming was in progress before one of the latter, made up to look like a big city bank. Uniformed police crouched behind swivelled cars, guns at the ready as two masked men emerged at the run. It looked real enough now; Nicola could well imagine the authenticity on screen.

The make-up department was a single-storeyed building containing several rooms. Once she had delivered her charge, Margot wished her luck and departed. Over the following hour, Nicola was made-up, had her hair combed and pinned into period style and was despatched to wardrobe a short distance away to be dressed in a long skirt and jacket which were far too warm for the climate. By the time she reached Stage Eight she was perspiring heavily, yet dared not wipe her face with a tissue for fear of removing most of the carefully applied foundation. The thought of the coming ordeal made her want to turn tail and run. It was only loyalty to Sam that kept her from doing so.

Sam *and* Ross—although the latter had been so distant these last few days. Several times she had been on the verge of asking him if he had changed his own mind about the coming test, but she had held her tongue. Stop vacillating, he had told her, so stop it she would. If he had anticipated a decision against rather than for, then he was out of luck.

He had wished her luck this morning. That at least was some comfort. There was a chance she might see him in the studio commissary during the lunch break if they got through in time. Whether she would know the decision by then was doubtful—unless she was so absolutely hopeless it was obvious to all without waiting for the print. Sam would be honest with her, if no one else was. He hadn't got where he was by soft-pedalling.

There had to be about thirty people waiting her arrival in the vast interior of the sound stage. Only one corner was illuminated, showing a set depicting what looked like the main room of a log-built ranch house. Sam was talking to a man Nicola recognised from their big party before Christmas. He broke off as she came tentatively forwards, beckoning her over.

'You remember Carl Foster?' he said. 'He's going to be directing *Sky*.'

Carl was small and thin and intense. From the way he looked at her, Nicola wondered if he had meant a word of what he had said that evening regarding her suitability for the role. In some strange way, the knowledge that he ws not as eager to have her in his picture as Sam himself so obviously was put her on her mettle—made her suddenly want to prove him wrong and Sam right. She even managed a smile as she shook hands.

'You studied the piece I marked for you?' asked Sam.

'Yes,' she said. 'I enjoyed the whole script.'

'That should make the writers happy,' commented the director on a dry note. 'Let's get it under way, shall we? If you'd go and stand on the taped line by the set door, while they light you . . .'

Standing there in that bright, hot circle, Nicola felt suddenly and wonderfully at home. It was different from a theatre stage, of course, but not all that different. There was even an audience to supply atmosphere—hard-bitten crew though they might be. She went over the short scene she was to play in her mind. Catherine was seeing her new home for the first time, realising just what she had given up. She only had a few lines of dialogue to speak, but the delivery was crucial. If she could just forget the camera, the heat, the watching eyes, and for a few short moments become that young woman, scarcely out of her teens and thousands of miles from home and family.

'OK,' said a voice. 'Let's go, Carl.'

'In your own time,' came the laconic instruction out of the dimness beyond the lights.

Nicola made no initial movement of limb, allowing her face to reveal the passing emotions as she slowly turned her head to survey the room before her. The long journey overland, the unaccustomed privations, they had all taken their toll. She had believed herself prepared for anything, ready to accept whatever came her way, providing Tyler was with her, but this—the place where she was to spend the rest of her life—was too much. She wanted so desperately to be home again, among the old and familiar. For one fleeting moment, she knew what it was to hate the man she loved for what he had done to her.

The moment passed, thrust into oblivion as her spirit reasserted itself. Chin lifting, she moved a step forward, speaking her lines with just the merest hint of a catch in her voice as she reassured Tyler that all was well.

It was the silence that brought her down to earth again. Flushing, she looked out at the sea of faces beyond the lights. Had she been that bad?

Sam was the first to speak. 'I guess I know a winner when I see one,' he said with satisfaction. 'What do *you* say, Carl?'

'I'll wait till I see the re-run,' said the director. 'That

wasn't a bad effort, Mrs King.'

'Not bad?' snorted the studio head. 'It was brilliant! I don't need to see any screenings. Get the casting office to fix a work permit. Time somebody in there earned their keep. Standard contract—and we're going to need photographs right away for the publicity guys. They'll need some background detail, Nicola.' He paused, shaking his head. 'Doesn't have the right sound. The King's OK, but I'd as soon go for a complete break. Any suggestions?'

It was Nicola's turn to shake her head, too bemused to think straight about anything. She was on her way! She could scarcely believe it. They hadn't even asked her to run through the scene again. I'm going to be in films, she thought—well, one film, at any rate. Whether there would be others remained to be seen.

One of the technicians gave her a thumbs-up. Suddenly she was laughing, tension released. 'How about Eve?' she said. 'Eve Sinclair.'

'Worth considering,' Sam agreed. 'I'll get somebody to take you across to photographic soon as you're changed. After that, come on back to the office. We'll have the paperwork ready and waiting. We might even find time for lunch, if we're lucky,' he added with a smile. 'Can't have you passing out on me now.'

Passing out was the last thing she felt like doing. There was too much to stay alert for. It wasn't going to be plain sailing, by any means. She had so much to learn about film work. Ross would be invaluable to her there—if he were willing. He had been on this route before.

It was almost two-thirty before anyone proposed lunch. Nicola found herself escorted across to the commissary by an entourage that included Margo McReath, but not Sam himself. There were few people left at the tables, and no sign of Ross. He would, Margo said, have long since returned to the set.

'Why not drop in and surprise him?' she suggested

lightly over coffee. 'He's out on Stage Twelve. I can get someone to run you over, if you like.'

Nicola's hesitation was brief. If she was going to be a part of this world of his, then what better than to take a look at what it was all about? 'I'd like that,' she said.

Margo commandeered one of the run-about jeeps for her. 'If the red light is on, it means they're going for a take,' she advised, 'so wait until it goes out before you open the door or you could finish up with a camera wrapped round your neck.' Her smile was friendly. 'I'm real glad you made it. This property means a lot to Mr Walker.'

Nicola smiled back. 'It's going to mean a lot to me, too.'

The red light *was* on at Stage Twelve. Nicola waved her young driver on his way and leaned against the lofty side of the building to wait, still trying to convince herself that the morning had not been yet another dream. Eve Sinclair! She wanted suddenly to laugh. It sounded like some character from a romantic novel! Still, Sam seemed to like it, and his was the final choice. It would look great in print, he had said; it had certainly looked good on the contract she had signed. Even allowing for the fact that as an unknown she was on the lower end of the fee scale, the amount she was to be paid had taken her breath away. She was no longer dependent on Ross, she realised. Not financially, at any rate. The fact alone gave her immeasurable confidence.

Above her head, the red light flicked out. She quickly opened the personnel door set within the huge sliding one, and slipped inside. The set was down towards the far end of the stage, the overhead lights so bright they dazzled her eyes as she made her way across. Cables stretched everywhere, treacherous to the unwary. One or two people glanced at her incuriously as she paused on the fringe of the group, but nobody spoke to her.

Nothing much seemed to be happening at present. From where she stood, she could see through between cameras and lights to the bedroom set. Ross was sitting on the end of the double bed, talking to Keir while Renata lay gazing into the rafters with a bored expression on her face. Despite the sheet across her waist, it was obvious that she was totally nude. Keir probably was too, thought Nicola, trying to keep a rational outlook. She had seen nude love scenes depicted on screen enough times, but what she had always assumed was that they were shot in as close to privacy as it was possible to get, with only those technicians around who were vital to the action. Not that anyone appeared to be paying much attention. For the most part they looked as bored as Renata herself.

Whatever Ross was saying, it seemed to be having impact on Keir, who was nodding as if in agreement. Renata didn't stir a muscle until Ross was on his feet and moving away, sitting up to fling a single vicious epithet at his departing back. With her dark hair tumbling about her shoulders, and breasts firmly thrust, she looked, Nicola thought, supremely alluring. Ross didn't even look round, his face impassive as he made for the canvas chair set to one side of the camera, in whose shadows Nicola stood.

He was almost on before he saw her, his expression undergoing a swift and unencouraging change.

'Been there long?' he asked.

'No.' Nicola was conscious of all eyes in the vicinity turned her way. 'I waited for the light to go out before I came in,' she added hastily.

'So I'd hope.' His glance shifted to a jean-clad youth carrying a clipboard. 'Find my wife a chair, will you, Pete?'

The stirring of interest was not imagined. Keir gave her a cheery wave from the bed. His co-star said something short and obviously nasty, receiving a blandly infuriating smile by way of reply. Nicola sat down in the chair placed beside the director's own, wishing fervently that she had stayed away. It took little perception to judge that her presence was unwelcome. Ross looked like a man with a lot on his mind.

The following hour was not one she would have wished to repeat. To say Ross ignored her would have been erroneous in the sense that he simply forgot she was there. It was Renata who seemed to respond to the fresh blood in the audience, turning in a performance that should have set the sheets themselves on fire. Keir responded magnificently. Watching the pair of them, Nicola for one could have sworn that here were two people passionately and uninhibitedly in love. The final 'cut and print' was a relief in more ways than one. If this was a taste of what might be expected of her in the not too distant future, they could forget it! There was no ways she could ever command enough detachment from the surroundings to play that kind of part.

Ross called it a day at that point, whether because she was there or because he had had enough was difficult to tell. Scarcely pausing to wrap herself in the robe held ready for her, Renata departed forthwith. Keir came over to where Nicola sat waiting for Ross to finish her discussion with a small group of technicians, the short robe securely belted around his waist.

'I seem to be making a habit of this,' he said, grin unabashed. 'Rumour has it you were taking a screen test this morning. How did it go?'

Ross had not mentioned the test. Nicola felt no compunction in making Keir first recipient of the news. 'I got the part I was up for.'

Blue eyes lit up. 'No kidding! Hey, that's great!' He lifted his voice to carry to those already moving off-set. 'Magnum just bought itself a new star!'

Congratulations were offered, sly glances cast in Ross's direction. He appeared not to have heard the announcement, but Nicola had seen his back suddenly stiffen. His own fault, she thought in self-justification.

All it would have taken was a word, a warming smile. If he didn't want her to do it, he shouldn't have pressed her into it.

Keir drifted off to get dressed. The arc lights were extinguished, leaving the odd bulb to show the way to the door. By the time Ross was finally ready to go, Nicola was on the verge of walking out and leaving him. She felt in the way; an encumbrance.

'Sorry about that,' he said shortly as they made their way outside into the fresh air. 'We normally hash things out over a beer in the commissary.'

'Don't let me stop you,' she said, equally short. 'I'm sure Sam will fix me a lift.'

'Not necessary. I said all I had to say back there.' There was a pause, a change of tone. 'I gather you came through with flying colours. That's great.'

'Is it?' Her face was averted. 'I didn't think you were all that interested.'

'Because I neglected to stop work in order to boost your ego?'

Nicola flushed. 'That wasn't what I meant.'

'That's what it sounded like.' He added levelly, 'I'd just scrapped take sixteen on that scene. The last thing I had in mind was your screen test right then.'

'That was more than obvious.' Her voice took on a note of scorn. 'I didn't realise you were into *that* kind of film!'

'What kind is that?'

'Pornography!'

His laugh was totally unexpected. 'They weren't doing anything we haven't done ourselves.'

'At the proper time and in the proper place,' she retorted with heat. 'Not on film, just to up the box-office receipts!'

Ross seized her arm, pulling her around to face him. He was angry himself now, his face set. 'It's about time you grew up,' he clipped. 'Try reading the script before you start telling me how to do my job!'

The hurt had gone too deep to allow for any backing down now. 'That's a cop-out, and you know it! If anybody should be against exploitation, you should. Look what happened to Arlene!'

The moment she had said it, Nicola wanted to bite off her tongue. His face had turned to stone, the grey eyes so cold they froze her to the marrow. She put a hand on his arm, desperate to right the wrong. 'Ross, I'm sorry. I didn't mean to say it.'

The coldness stayed. 'Why not, if that's what you feel? One of these days you're going to realise that being sorry doesn't automatically cancel the event..'

'I know that now.' She felt wretched. 'I said it off the top of my head without thinking. I said it all off the top of my head. Just don't keep looking at me like that.'

If there was any return of expression at all, it was weariness. 'I guess I'm as much to blame. You merit every accolade.'

'Only not there and not then.' She laid her face against his chest, oblivious of any possible passers-by. 'I was jealous, I suppose.'

He was holding her, though not tightly. 'Who of?'

'Not who—what.' She raised rueful blue eyes, searching his for a glimmer of understanding. 'You're so wrapped up in your work, Ross. I feel . . . left out.'

'You're going to have a career of your own to keep you busy,' he said. 'That should sort it out.' He dropped a light, totally impersonal kiss on the end of her nose and put her away from him. 'New Year's Eve tomorrow. We'll both make resolutions then. For now, it's time we went home.'

He hadn't forgiven her, Nicola thought numbly. Not wholly. But then she couldn't say she had totally forgiven him. It was to be hoped that the coming year would see a closing of the gulf which yawned between them.

CHAPTER NINE

THEY saw the New Year in quietly, much to Nicola's relief. She had been anticipating yet another of the interminable Hollywood parties, with the Press in attendance, hoping for some scandal to report. Disregarding the warmth of the evening, Ross lit a fire in the living-room's open hearth after dinner, handing Nicola a bag of chestnuts with a light remark about achieving at least part of the dream.

'Couldn't manage the snow,' he added, watching her face as she opened the bag. 'Or the robins either, if it comes to that. But then, I'm only a director, not a props manager.'

Things had been better between them today. Enough so to infuse real feeling into the kiss she moved impulsively to give him.

'I'd rather have these than a bag of diamonds!' she claimed extravagantly, and heard his laugh ring out.

'That,' he declared, 'has to make you just about unique in this town!' The grey eyes looking down at her had a questing expression. 'No more uncertainties?'

Plenty, she wanted to tell him, but the words wouldn't come. She smiled instead, shaking her head. 'No more uncertainties.'

Something in him seemed to relax. 'Good. How about I make us a drink while you put those to roast?' He was moving as he spoke. 'Just three hours to go and we'll be into the new year. We may as well enjoy what's left of the old.'

It was going to be a hard year, Nicola told herself, kneeling before the leaping flames to spread the chestnuts along the hot stone. She had a career as well as a marriage to work at. This coming month was going to be the worst part—although she would at least have plenty to occupy both mind and body. What she really wanted, she supposed, was for Ross to be right there with her on the set of *The Same Sky* instead of Carl Foster. Not that he would want it, even if the opportunity had been there. He might have urged her into making the decision, but that was as far as his involvement went; he had already made that clear. This time, Svengali was opting out.

She hadn't heard his return with the drinks. The first she knew of his closeness was when she sat back on her heels to screw up the empty bag, and felt his hand touch her shoulder. When she turned, he was kneeling right behind her, the firelight glinting in his eyes.

'Hows about we let the New Year in early?' he said softly. 'I don't think I can wait three hours.'

The heat at her back was as nothing compared with that rising in her. She went blindly into his arms, meeting his mouth with eagerness, with passion, with a fervent desire to make the occasion memorable for them both. He undressed her slowly, pausing to kiss each portion of soft flesh he uncovered, devouring her with lips and tongue and teeth until she moaned for relief. The firelight flickered over his body when he stood up to slide out of his own clothes, and, looking at him, she was reminded of that very first night they had made love. She had loved him then and she loved him now. It was his deeper emotions she still couldn't be sure of.

She spread supple limbs to take him into her, wrapping him close, relishing his weight. His hands were buried in her hair, his lips feathering kisses over her eyes, her temple, down the side of her cheek to find her mouth. She could feel him inside her, part of her, possessing her, feel the rug thick and soft beneath her. When he started to move it was slowly at first, almost languidly, the power in his loins held in check until he sensed her readiness. Fulfilment was total, the most wonderful, complete experience in her life. She knew it all now, she thought mistily, lying satiated in the close, warm circle of his arms.

It was Ross who moved first, lifting his head to look at the clock in the alcove. 'Nearly two and a half hours still to go,' he murmured. 'We'll do that again, as soon as I've recovered some strength! In the meantime,' he added with a smile down into her eyes, 'I think your chestnuts are burning.'

They weren't on their own, Nicola reflected as he rolled away to reach for the tongs. She felt stoked up with new hope. She and Ross were going to make it. They had to make it. Let Paula find her own man. This one was hers!

The film company left for San Francisco on the second of January. Nicola accompanied Ross to the airport in order to drive the car home again.

'You can find your way back OK?' he asked when his bags had been handed into the keeping of a porter.

'If not today, tomorrow,' she said, and laughed. 'I'll cope.'

'Sure you will.' He looked at her for a long moment, an odd expression in his eyes, 'I'll ring you when I can. Take care of yourself, Nicola.'

His kiss left her aching. There was so much she wanted to tell him, and none of it germane to the moment. Already Ross's thoughts were winging ahead, concentrating on the work he loved so much better than he would probably love any woman. At the best, she only held a minor share in his life. It was going to be a long, long month until she saw him again.

The route back was easy enough in theory, once she got herself on to Lincoln and heading in the right direction. Driving the Mercedes was child's play, however, compared with negotiating the Los Angeles traffic. Inevitably she found herself in the wrong lane, missed the turning out to the Pacific Highway and was forced to turn right on to Santa Monica.

Reviewing the situation in her mind's eye, she reckoned that if she made a left at the next intersection she would arrive at Sunset eventually, and from there could make a way back down to the coast road. Short of turning round and retracing her route—hardly feasible—or carrying on into downtown LA, there was no other choice.

Like most roads in the American grid system, the one she chose was long and straight, with high-strung traffic lights seemingly every few hundred yards. Stopped at the first one by a red, she was aware out of the corner of her eye of an open tourer drawing up alongside, but paid no heed to the occupant until the horn was blown.

Blond hair ruffled by the breeze, and a devil-may-care smile on his lips, Keir gesticulated to her to let down her window.

'I'm on my way to eat,' he called across. 'How about joining me?'

The lights changed before she could answer. Keir was first away, cutting in front of her and making signs for her to follow him. As if, Nicola thought drily, she had been left with much choice! Three city block further on, he signalled a turn, slowing right down to make sure she was with him before swinging into the forecourt of a Red Lobster restaurant.

There was room to park side by side. Getting out of the car, he came across to open her door, leaning on it to study her appreciatively. 'You drive nearly as well as you look,' he said.

Nicola laughed. 'You're overplaying your line.'

'The story of my life.' He indicated the restaurant doors. 'Not quite Ma Maison, but the seafood special is second to none. If you don't fancy fish, they do a pretty good steak.'

She had to eat some time, Nicola reflected in amusement. It might as well be in company. 'Fish will be fine,' she said. She gave him a swift glance as memory caught up with her. 'Aren't you supposed to be in San Francisco?'

'I'm not needed for a couple of days,' he returned easily. 'No point in hanging around. Matter of fact, I was thinking of running out to pay a visit this afternoon.'

'On me?'

'Who else?'

She said after a moment, 'Because Ross is away?'

'That could have something to do with it.' He held open the door for her, blue eyes very direct. 'I think there's something you should know about that husband of yours.'

Nicola returned his look as levelly. 'I know everything I need to know.'

'Maybe. There's only one way to find out.'

He didn't open up on the subject until they were seated, with their order on its way. Even then it was Nicola herself who had to do the prompting. 'So what is it you think I might not know?'

Keir seemed to consider his words for a moment. When he did speak, she had a feeling he was hedging. 'You'd heard how his wife died?'

'Yes.' She added succinctly, 'He told me all of it before we were married. And if you're going to say some people still think he had something to do with her death, then you can tell them from me to go climb a tree!'

His shrug made light of the moment. 'I guess nobody really believes that any more—although turning up again with another wife in tow doesn't exactly suggest he was overburdened with grief, either.'

'If that were true,' she defended, 'why would he have gone away at all?'

'To give it time to blow over. Just the way it has.' There was a pause, a change of tone. 'I might have said to escape Paula Reddington's clutches into the bargain, except that present events don't bear that theory out.'

Nicola stared at him, heartbeats suddenly heavier. 'What are you getting at?'

The shrug came again. 'It's pretty common knowledge that he and Reddington were having an affair before Arlene died. Could be part of the reason he was pulled in for questioning over her death.'

She had to believe him, Nicola thought numbly. It bore out so much that she had suspected. But it was in the past, she emphasised, trying to be rational about it, and no worse than what Arlene herself had been doing. Except . . . Her eyes focused afresh on Keir's face. 'What did you mean by "present events"?'

'It's started up again,' he said. 'They've been seen together.'

It was difficult to draw breath—even more so to speak. 'I don't believe it!'

There was an expression in the eyes opposite that seemed to mirror her pain. 'Why didn't Ross take you with him?'

'Because his schedule is too tight to allow for much free time. You should be able to understand that.'

Keir's gaze didn't leave her face. 'Supposing I told you that Paula Reddington left town yesterday.'

'To go where?' Nicola challenged.

'Ah, now that's the sixty-four-thousand-dollar question. Coincidental, wouldn't you say?'

Yes, she thought bleakly. *Too* coincidental. Whatever resolutions Ross had made for the New Year, they didn't have to include giving up old habits. Why assume that a man who made love the way he did was going to be satisifed with one woman? 'Why tell me?' she asked on a dull note. 'Why not leave me in ignorance?'

Keir replied softly. 'Because you deserve a better deal than you're getting. You're out of a different mould, Nicola.'

Ross had used those very words, she remembered, fighting to stay on top of the anguish. She looked without interest at the loaded plate put before her by the waitress, pushing it away with a jerky hand. 'I'm sorry, I'm not hungry any more. If you don't mind, I'll go on back——' she couldn't bring herself to say 'home' '—to the house.'

'I'll come with you,' Keir offered, but she shook her head.

'I don't need any shoulder to cry on, thanks.' She gave him a hardened glance as she rose to her feet. 'You should have remembered that the bearer of bad news was never a popular figure.'

'I did,' he said wryly. 'A risk I had to take. Believe it or not, I had your best interests at heart.'

'I'm sure you did.' She left him sitting there.

She never reached Sunset Boulevard, for the simple reason that the road she was on didn't stretch that far out. By turning left on San Vincente, then right on to Entrada, she eventually arrived at the Coastal Highway, heading for Malibu because there was nowhere else to go right now.

She didn't doubt what Keir had told her. Ross might enjoy making love to her, but he didn't love her. He never had loved her in any lasting fashion. This town, their way of life—none of it was conducive to a lasting emotion. The question now was where she went from here. She had her career, of course. That had to be worth a deal of heartache. Eve Sinclair, star! What else did she need?

She was kidding herself, and she knew it. Nothing could compensate for what she had lost. Except that one couldn't lose what one had never really had, came the thought. Ross was his own man. He always would be his own man. Not even Paula could alter that fact.

His phone call that same evening did nothing to alter her mood. Allaying suspicion, she assumed with a cynicism newly acquired. She spoke to him coolly, impersonally, sensing his uncertainty through the long pauses.

'Are you feeling OK?' he asked at one point. 'You sound so . . . remote.'

Nicola laughed, the sound harsh to her own ears. 'I *am* remote. Several hundred miles remote! How did it go today?'

'We're set up and ready to roll. The treadmill starts as soon as the light's right for the bridge scene.'

'Is Renata still playing up?'

'In that way, she's entirely reliable.' There was silence again. Faintly, in the background, Nicola heard another voice—a woman's voice. 'I'm needed,' said Ross. 'It might be a couple of days before I get to ring you again.'

'Supposing I wanted to ring you?' she asked, and could hear the hesitation.

'Might be difficult. We'll be running the dailies through in the evenings.'

'I'll leave it to you, then,' she said. 'Goodnight, Ross.'

She stood for several moments, listening numbly to the burr of the replaced receiver at the far end of the line before slowly replacing her own. There was no conclusive proof; she must keep telling herself that. There were female crew members. She must learn to keep an open mind.

She learned a lot over the following days, not all of it easy to accept. Along with her new screen name went a whole new past, hinting at aristocratic connections. Every major newspaper allotted column space to the story. 'British Actress Steals Plum Role,' said one, 'Magnum Signs Unknown,' said another. Two leading magazines requested exclusive interviews—both refused on the grounds that a little elusiveness would do her image no harm. That was one decision with which Nicola could whole-heartedly concur.

It had taken her three days to come to any final conclusion where Ross was concerned. Three days, during which she had undergone agonies of uncertainty. He had phoned her again—a conversation so normal she had almost been convinced that everything was all right. Almost, but not quite. Finding Paula Reddington's unlisted home number in his personal directory had jolted her back to reality. Miss Reddington was out of town, the maid had said, and not expected back until the end of the month.

So that was that. The evidence was too damning. The very next day she found herself a small apartment in Brentwood and moved in. It came fully furnished: bedroom, bathroom, well-equipped kitchen, nice living area and balcony with fine view. The cost wasn't low, but on what she was being paid she could afford it, she reckoned. This was only the beginning, Sam had promised. If *The Same Sky* proved the success he predicted she was on her way to the top.

It had been necessary to advise the casting office of her change of address, of course. Whether the information had been passed on to Sam himself she had no way of knowing. She spent most of her time at the studio, have wardrobe fittings, make-up tests, familiarising herself with the filmworld terminology. Most evenings, she studied the script, trying to imagine what it was going to be like playing it scene by scene, and not even in logical order.

The rest of the cast were all experienced, her co-star, Dean Westwood, a veteran whose previous films had all done well at the box office. He was at present on vacation, and not due to return until the day before they started shooting, which meant they would meet for the first time on-set—a prospect Nicola viewed with some trepidation. It was important, to her mind, that they form some kind of rapport if the love scenes were to be convincing. He was older than she was by some ten years, but still well capable of playing a man in his mid-twenties. Something of a loner, by all accounts.

There was no word from Ross, although he must know by now that she had left the house. Nicola could summon little emotion. From now on, she lived only for her career. It was less likely to fall about her ears.

Shooting started on January the fifteenth. On the twenty-fifth a reporter from the *Los Angeles Times* called to ask if Eve Sinclair was in fact the present wife of director Ross King. There was no point in denying something that could so easily be verified. Not much use, either, in appealing to the man not to print the story, though she tried it, anyway. It made the following morning's edition, half a column of snide innuendo that made her curl up inside.

'I didn't set out to use Ross, but nobody's going to believe it after this,' she told Dean Westwood over lunch in the commissary. 'They even had to rake up all that stuff about Arlene again.'

'And in a couple of days it will all be forgotten again,' he assured her. 'That's what *you've* got to do—forget it.'

Nicola looked at the dark, ruggedly handsome man

who had become friend as well as occasional mentor over this past couple of weeks, thinking with a pang how much he reminded her of Ross. He was right, of course. A blind eye and a deaf ear were prime requisites in this line. She said obliquely, 'Were you ever married, Dean?'

'Twice,' he acknowledged. 'Both disasters. Women are hell to live with.'

'That's a sweeping statement.'

'Based on experience.' He shrugged. 'Or maybe I just wasn't cut out for marriage. One thing I do know, I shan't be trying it again. A bachelor pad, freedom to come and go with no questions asked, that's my idea of the good life!' He glanced up at the clock on the far wall. 'We'd better get back on set. Carl was bad enough this morning, without keeping him hanging around.'

'My fault,' Nicola said ruefully. 'I couldn't seem to do anything right.'

Dean shook his head. 'He's been on a short fuse since we started shooting. And have you noticed his colour recently? If I were a medic, I'd go for the liver.'

'If he was taken ill, what would happen to the film?' Nicola asked. 'We're supposed to be leaving for Texas the week after next.'

'They'd have to bring someone else in to finish it.' He gave her an encouraging grin. 'Cheer up. I'm a born pessimist.'

Studying the director between takes that afternoon, Nicola thought the initial assessment was probably right. Carl looked ill. If she hadn't noticed it before, it was only because her whole attention had been concentrated on acquitting herself well in this her first role. Working with Carl had been no picnic, but better the devil one knew. A change now could ruin everything.

With a make-up call for six o'clock each morning, late

nights were a thing of the past. She was usually in bed by nine, going over the next day's scheduled scenes before falling asleep. Carl Foster was far from a one-take director. Every scene would be repeated four or five times, with minor adjustments, shot from different angles, agonised over in the screening-room. Nicola had seen the daily rushes on two occasions, then left them to it, unable to assess her own performance objectively when the storyline itself had no cohesion. When it was finished and edited she might watch it; then, again, she might not. Public opinion was all that really mattered in the end.

She was undressed, and in the middle of making herself a bedtime drink that evening when the security telephone buzzed. She ignored it the first time, thinking that someone had pressed the wrong button in error, but the second ring was too insistent.

Frowning, she went to lift the receiver, said shortly, 'I think you must have a wrong number.'

The voice on the other end of the line was equally cool. 'Not this time.'

Breath caught in her throat, she said, 'Ross?'

'Who else?' He waited a moment, as if in anticipation, before adding, 'Do I get to come up?'

'Of course.' Nervelessly, she pressed the door release, hanging up again to stand chewing her lower lip while she tried to compose herself. The month wasn't yet up; she hadn't expected he would be back in town for several more days. She had seen nothing of Sam personally, nor had she heard from Velma since her move, yet the information regarding her whereabouts had most likely been provided by the former. What she was going to say to him she had no idea. He had sounded so cold, so clipped. What she had to remember was that he was the one who had set the wheels in motion.

So stay off the defensive, she told herself.

There was no time to fling on some clothes. He had seen her in less many times, anyway. Nevertheless, she found herself tying the belt of her light robe more securely about her waist as she went to open the apartment door to his ring.

It had been less than a month since she had last seen him; if felt more like a year. Looking into those taut, lean features, she wanted suddenly to fling herself into his arms, to tell him she didn't care, to do anything that would wipe away the distance between them and put things back the way they had been. It took all her acting skill to cover her emotions and say steadily, 'You'd better come in.'

She closed the door again before turning to face him. He was wearing denim jeans and a light sweater, but there was nothing casual about the look in the grey eyes.

'Sam's right about one thing,' he said. 'You can act a part. Only why bother with all that shall-I-shan't-I claptrap?'

Nicola stared at him, the wind taken out of her sails. 'What are you talking about?'

His lip curled. 'It's a bit late to start playing the injured innocent. You barely let me get out of town before you moved out. You'd got what you wanted— the thing you've been angling for all along. Marriage too restrictive for you, was it?'

'Don't you try to turn this thing round on me!' She was trembling, but with anger rather than impotence. 'I wasn't prepared to be made a complete fool of, that's all!'

One dark eyebrow lifted sardonically. '*Me* make a fool of *you?*'

'You know what I'm talking about.'

'Suppose you lay it on the line for me.'

She said it softly. 'Paula Reddington.'

There was no discernible change of expression. 'So?'

'Stop it, Ross!' She was fast losing patience with this whole situation. 'Let's cut out the playacting from both sides, shall we? You didn't want me with you in San Francisco because you'd already arranged to meet Paula there.'

'Is that a fact?'

'You know it is.' She hadn't moved away from the door, because to do so meant passing him. 'You were having an affair with her when Arlene died. Everybody knew that. I'm not sure why you married me—impulse, probably—but it all started to change when you saw her again. Well, if she's what you want, you can have her. Only you can't have me, too!'

'No go, honey.' His tone was flat. 'You married me in the hope of furthering your career. Well, you succeeded. Congratulations!'

'It wasn't like that.' Her voice had acquired a slight tremor. 'If it had been, don't you think I'd have jumped at Sam's offer the first time he made it?'

'I think,' he said hardily, 'that you're shrewd enough to realise a little seeming reluctance would only make him more determined to have you. Not that I'm knocking your talent. You have to be good to make that much of an impression on him.'

She swallowed thickly. 'You've been in touch with Sam?'

'He was the one who told me where you were after I'd spent forty-eight hours trying to contact you.'

'It didn't occur to you to come and find out why I'd moved out, of course,' she flashed. 'Too busy, were you?'

'Something like that.' There was no hint of apology in his voice. 'I asked Sam to leave you alone till I'd seen you. I gather he took me at my word.' He paused, his expression unrevealing. 'Who told you about Paula?'

Somewhere deep down in the recesses of her mind there must have lingered a faint spark of doubt, Nicola thought. Otherwise it couldn't hurt so much to hear him admit it now. 'Does it matter?' she asked dully. 'It probably worked out for the best, anyway. I could have let this chance slip through my fingers and still finished up getting dumped. This way, we both have what we want.'

'Not altogether.' Ross spoke quietly, but there was a dangerous spark in his eyes. 'I think you owe me a final gesture—call it rent in arrears, if you like. What time are you on call in the morning?'

'I have to be at the studio for six.' Nicola could feel her heart thudding against her ribcage. 'Why?'

His smile had a cruel edge. 'I'd have thought that went without question. I'm spending the night here.'

'No, you're not!' The anger spreading through her had an element of desperation at its core. 'I owe you nothing, Ross. Nothing! Just get out!'

He ignored her, turning away to cast a cynical glance around the room. 'Nice little place. Kingsized bed, I hope?'

'Stop it!' This time, it was almost an appeal. 'Do you think you're the only one whose pride took a battering? I spent three days trying to convince myself I was wrong about you. That last time you called me very nearly did it, too.'

He swung again to look at her, the hardness still there about his mouth. 'So what finally did the trick?'

'I found Paula's private number in your little black book. Her maid said she was out of town until the end of the month.'

'And?'

Her head was up, her eyes challenging. 'What else was necessary?'

'You could have asked where she'd gone, for one thing.'

She stared at him for a long moment, trying vainly to pierce the steel. 'You're trying to tell me it wasn't San Francisco?'

'I'm not trying to tell you anything. You already made up your mind. Well, so did I. And I'm not leaving here until I've had full satisfaction. You can supply it willingly or unwillingly—that's up to you.'

Nicola said slowly, 'You think I'd be reluctant to call for help because of the publicity, is that it? Just try what you're suggesting, and see!'

The jeering smile came again. 'If this place is built the way it should be, you could scream your head off and it wouldn't get through the proofing. Speaking of publicity, that was quite a piece *The Times* ran on the two of us.'

She was trying hard to conceal her emotions. 'I'm sorry they dragged past history into it. I suppose it was inevitable under the circumstances. I can hardly be blamed for that.'

'Like I said, you're a pretty shrewd cookie.' Ross used the term with derisive deliberation. 'You're also pretty good in bed, if my memory doesn't fail me. If you're due up at five or thereabouts, then we should maybe get to it. Which is the bedroom?'

He had her in a cleft stick, Nicola acknowledged numbly. Dressed the way she was, she could scarcely flee the apartment, and it was most probably true about the sound-proofing. Certainly, she never heard anything of her neighbours.

'Don't just stand there,' he said. 'Lead the way.'

'Find it yourself,' she retorted on a note of contempt.

'Passive resistance, is it?' He shot out a sudden hand and grasped her wrist, lips twisting at her quickly suppressed reaction. 'You don't believe I'll go through with it, do you? I'm going to enjoy convincing you, Nicola.'

It was difficult not to struggle against him as he led her with unerring instinct to the bedroom. The curtains had not yet been drawn on the scintillating view over the city.

'I'll settle for moonlight,' he said, letting go of her to pull the sweater over his head in one swift movement. 'Take your things off—unless you'd rather I did it for you.'

She wasn't going to fight him, she vowed numbly. If this was his way of showing her how little he cared for her feelings, then let him get on with it. Steeling herself, she pulled open the tie belt of her robe and slid the garment from her shoulders, letting it drop to the floor. The air-conditioning was turned off, she knew, yet she felt chilled through.

'Everything,' Ross insisted.

Without looking at him, Nicola jerked the thin straps of her nightdress down her arms, stepping out of the filmy little pile at her feet and moving over to slide between crisp cotton sheets. A moment later, Ross got into the bed from the other side. She felt the brush of his bare thigh as he seized the sheet that covered her and drew it down the full length of her body, and was unable to control the quivering of her limbs.

'I'm cold,' she whispered.

'Not for long,' he said.

He put his lips to her breast, running the very tip of his tongue aound the outer edge of the areola. The sensation created was exquisite—a pleasure close to pain. It made her want to writhe, to gasp, to take his head between her hands and tear him away, yet at the same time to hold him there, to feel his mouth moving over her flesh. It had been so long; she hadn't realised just how much she had missed this, how much she had missed him. She had to forcibly remind herself of his reasons for being here with her at all. Reasons that nothing could excuse. If she gave in to him, if she let her body respond to him the way it so desperately wanted to, then she was equally degenerate.

As if sensing what was in her mind, he left her breasts and laid a slow trail of kisses from the hollow of her throat along the side of her neck to her jawline, hardly more than a brushing of the lips, yet devastating in effect. He moved on top of her as he found her mouth, sliding his hands into the thickness of her hair, his thumbs gently stroking the soft skin just behind her earlobes, until every nerve in her body was quivering uncontrollably.

'Put your hands on me,' he commanded softly.

She did so because she couldn't help herself, thrilling to the hard muscularity. Her lips softened, parted, began to answer. She was being a fool, but at this moment she didn't care. She wanted him so much, so very, very much! When they came together, it was as if they had never been apart.

She was lying on her side with her face burrowed in the pillow when he left the bed. Opening her eyes, she saw him silhouetted against the window as he pulled on his clothes. Throat tight, she could find no words. None, at least, that signified.

He left without speaking, although she sensed that he knew she was watching him. He had had what he had come for. Debt paid. If a part of her still yearned for him, then that was her hard lines.

CHAPTER TEN

CARL FOSTER collapsed on set two days later. This was one of those times, Dean commented ruefully when a diagnosis of acute hepatitis was confirmed, that he wished he could have been wrong. Even allowing for a full recovery, the director was going to be out of action for several weeks.

For forty-eight hours, no one seemed to know what was to happen. When asked, Sam himself could only say that all efforts were being made to secure the services of a replacement who was not only on Carl Foster's technical level, but close enough in style and technique to make the join as inconspicuous as possible. The main problem being, Nicola realised for herself, that such people were rarely to be found hanging around with free time on their hands. Ross, thank heaven, would be up to his eyes in post-production.

Meanwhile, Carl's assistant, Miles Randell, did his best, but it was obvious even to Nicola that he lacked the experience to step into the other man's shoes. Though there had been times when she had come close to hating Carl Foster for his sharp tongue and cruel wit, she felt he had also been capable of drawing from her that extra something which breathed real life into her role. Robbed of his presence, she could feel herself losing it.

'You're worrying too much,' Dean assured her. 'You're all tensed up and nervy because you've convinced yourself that Carl was the only one who could get you through, but if it's there in you at all, then you can bring it out yourself. Only for God's sake, relax!'

They were in the comfortably furnished dressing-room that was Nicola's personal retreat when she wasn't actually needed on set. She looked up now from her study of the shooting schedule with a wry little smile.

'It's all very well for you to talk. You've been in the business long enough to know exactly what you're doing. Carl could always tell me just where I was going wrong.'

'Sometimes to extremes.' Dean made a semi-apologetic gesture at the startled look in her eyes. 'He'd got you like a puppet on a string. If he'd said Catherine should dance a can-can in scene thirty-eight, you'd have given it your best shot!'

She had to laugh despite herself. 'That's totally untrue!'

'OK, so maybe you'd have kicked up at that——' he dodged the cushion she aimed at him '—but it's close enough.' He sobered to add, 'You're an actress, Nicola. A good actress. We all of us need direction or there'd be no shape, but the character is yours. Don't let anyone bully you into altering your interpretation.'

'I'll try,' she said. 'Do you think the new director—whoever he might be—will want to shoot the last couple of days' work again?'

'Could be. Depends how far over budget it would take us.' He waited for a moment before adding levelly, 'How are you going to react if they bring in Ross King?'

Her eyes widened again, in shock this time. 'He isn't available.'

'Dare say he could be if offered enough incentive. It isn't absolutely essential for the director to be involved in every facet of post-production. Grayling can be trusted to bring in the answer print on his own.'

'I couldn't work with him,' Nicola stated. 'Not the

way things are between us.'

'That's what I'd thought you'd say.' Dean leaned forward, the better to emphasise his words. 'Look, kid, you don't have director approval any more than I do, and you're in no position to start indulging in artistic temperament. What goes on between you and him in private has damn-all to do with what we're doing here. He's one of the best at his job. He could turn *Sky* into a top-rate film. If you're going to let personal feelings come before that, you're in the wrong profession.'

She bit her lip, knowing he was right. She hadn't told him, of course, about the other night, but it made no difference, anyway. If Ross came on-set tomorrow, then she had to regard him in a purely professional light. No doubt he would be more than capable of doing the same where she was concerned.

'Thanks,' she said, and smiled a little. 'I guess I needed that.'

A rap on the door was accompanied by a brief, 'Mr Westwood on set, please.' Dean came to his feet, looking down for a moment at the face still upturned to him, a certain reget in the line of his mouth. 'You've a whole lot to offer the right man, Nicola. If I'd met someone like you ten years ago, I might have had a different view of the female sex as a whole.'

Nicola sat for several minutes after he had left, trying to rationalise her emotions. Dean had almost certainly been warning her that the suggested deal was about to become fact; he always seemed to know what was going on before anyone else. Which meant that, either tomorrow or the next day, she was going to be called upon to act two parts. She could only hope and trust she would be capable of separating the one from the other.

The cast and crew of *The Same Sky* were given the news *en masse* that same evening. For the most part,

Nicola noted, it appeared to be received with relief, even anticipation, although sly glances were cast her way to see how she was taking it. She kept her own expression strictly neutral.

She spent the night in a state of tension, both dreading the morning, yet wanting to get it over, too. A part of her half anticipated a call from Ross himself, although what they could have to discuss, apart from divorce, she wasn't wholly sure. His contempt for her had been amply delineated the other night.

What she really wanted, she supposed wryly, was a temporary truce of a kind—an agreement to put their personal problems aside and concentrate on the job in hand. In all probability, that was something Ross would already have decided upon, but it would have helped to hear him say it.

Make-up and hair-dressing took an hour every morning. Having ascertained which scene they would be shooting first, by reference to the daily schedule, Nicola was then free to retire to her dressing-room and don the appropriate costume. It was continuity's job to check the detail, so that there would be no visible evidence of any pause in filming the sequence, but Nicola liked to keep her own inventory as an extra safeguard. Many was the time she had seen bits and pieces of clothing or accessories seemingly appearing or disappearing during what was purported to be a concurrent scene on the cinema screen.

She was running over this list prior to getting into the Edwardian evening gown which Catherine would wear in the form of premature 'women's lib' protest over the restrictions imposed by her new life-style, when the tap came on the door. Too early for the call boy, she thought, glancing at the wall clock prominently displayed. The only other person likely to pay her a visit before the day's work got under way in earnest was

Dean. It was like him, she reflected, to offer a word or two of comfort and reassurance, knowing how she must be feeling this morning.

Her smile of welcome faded abruptly when she opened the door to see Ross standing there. He was wearing jeans and a white T-shirt, the latter outlining the muscular structure of his chest and upper arms. Nicola found difficulty in bringing her eyes back to his face, feeling her colour rise at the sardonic expression.

'Expecting someone else?' he asked. 'Sorry to disappoint you. I thought we should clear the air some before we got started.' He drifted a downwards glance over her robe, his mouth taking on an added slant. 'It isn't going to take long.'

'You'd better come in,' she said.

He did so, leaning his back against the door in an attitude totally unreminiscent of her own tense stance the last time they had met. 'If we're going to work together,' he said, 'it has to be without any undercurrents. So, if you've anything you want to say, do it now.'

'I think we said all there was to say the other night,' Nicola replied shortly. 'In any case, I don't have any intention of letting our personal affairs intrude on our working relationship. If I fail to measure up in any way, all you have to do is tell me.'

'I'll do that OK.' There was a unnerving glint in his eyes. 'Judging from the dailies, I'll be doing a whole lot of it.'

'If you mean the last two days, that's hardly a fair assessment,' she declared with heat. 'Miles did his best, but . . .'

'It isn't Miles we're talking about, though, is it? Your performance hardly comes up to scratch.'

Blue eyes blazed at him. 'Don't try getting at me that way, Ross! Carl was . . .'

'I'm not Carl Foster.' He hadn't raised his voice at all,

but the inflection was harder. 'What satisfied him isn't necessarily going to satisfy me. You walked into this part on the strength of Sam's recommendation. You're going to play it the way he visualised it when he bought the property.'

She was breathing hard with the effort of keeping her temper. 'You're saying Carl Foster is second-rate, is that it?'

'No, that isn't it! I'm saying we have a different interpretation. Most of what you've done so far can be edited in, at a pinch, but the last two days' scenes will have to be re-shot. And don't lay the blame on Miles again,' he added, as she opened her mouth to speak. 'He did his best to hold it together.'

She said with bitterness, 'I bet I'm the only one of the cast you've spoken to like this.'

'You're the only one who's still wet behind the ears,' came the unmoved response. 'This isn't like theatre, where you can vary a performance from night to night; you have to sustain the same character over the whole shoot. Nobody's saying it's easy, but if you want to be a movie star——' he used the term with sarcasm '—then you'd better learn to take the knocks as well as the accolades. You've got it in you to be good in this part, providing you stop overplaying it.'

'Sam said I was brilliant in it,' Nicola defended, and wished she hadn't as she saw his lip curl afresh.

'Sam's so besotted with the whole idea of having you play the part, he'd turn a blind eye to any defect. He isn't happy with the rushes, but you're the last person he'd lay the blame on.' He registered the sudden sparkle in her eyes with an intolerant movement of his head. 'Let's dispense with the tears. I've been down that path too many times to give a damn. If you've got half the guts I think you have, you'll take it on the chin and come up fighting.'

The sparkle dried, giving way to icy fury. 'Like this?' she asked, and hit him with all her strength across the face.

In the moment following, she saw the red marks appear as if by magic against the tan of his skin, saw his jawline set so rigidly, the bone showed white at the points. Her own hand was hurting enough to bring moisture back to her eyes. She blinked rapidly to clear them, feeling the shamed reaction spreading through her.

'Ross . . .' she began thickly.

'Save it,' he advised. His tone was clipped, curt, wholly alienated. 'I should have left you back there in that damned jungle and saved us both a lot of hassle. I don't care how you feel about me personally, but you're not letting Sam down. If I have to take you apart and build you up again, I'll do it! I want you on set in ten minutes.'

She watched him go, aware of the futility in further appeal. She had acted like some dated, celluloid heroine, and she hated herself for it.

I'll show him, she vowed, trying to find some mitigation in all the things he had said to her. I'll show them all!

A film company on location can number as many as sixty people in all. The crew and cast of *The Same Sky* took over almost all available accommodation in the small, westernised town of Fort Livingdon.

Nicola was allocated a cabin at one of the three motels, next door to a woman who played her mother-in-law in the film. The latter was an actress named Rita Fleming, whom Nicola had admired for years. The relationship between them was amicable enough on the surface, although Dean had warned Nicola of the other's jealous streak where younger, up-and-coming actresses were concerned. There had been one or two incidents, earlier, when Carl Foster had been in the director's chair, but not since Ross had taken over. He was too much the man in command.

Neither Nicola's working nor her personal life had been easy since the day Ross had stepped into Carl's shoes. She ended each day almost too exhausted to eat. That first weekend, they had all put in overtime, reshooting the scenes Ross had outlined as essential. His direction, she had discovered, was far less abrasive than Carl's, even where she was concerned. He would take time and trouble to put across what it was he wanted, to suggest a change of inflection here, a movement there. Gradually and grudgingly, as the days passed, she had been forced to acknowledge not just an improved grasp of character in her own right, but a new sense of togetherness in the whole company.

'He hasn't altered the concept so much as refined it,' said Dean over an after-dinner drink that first evening in the motel. 'Carl lacks the subtle touch. Good thing Ross didn't kill Arlene. He couldn't have done much directing behind bars.'

He had been behind bars when she had first met him, Nicola thought. She glanced across to where he sat, deep in discussion with several members of the production team. They had all travelled down on the same plane, but he had made no attempt to come near her. Apart from on set, she never saw him. He was still living out at the beach, that much she did know. She felt a pang at the memories that thought conjured up. Even without Paula, it wouldn't have lasted, she told herself. There had been too much against them.

As if sensing her regard, Ross looked up and across, and for a moment or two their eyes met and held. Nicola was the first to look away, unable to maintain her cool composure.

'I think I'll turn in,' she said to Dean. 'It's going to be a heavy day tomorrow.'

'Starting with scene twenty-eight, aren't we?' He grinned at her. 'Ever fallen off a horse before?'

'Yes, I have,' she admitted wryly, her mind going back to Venezuela, but she firmly wrenched it back to the present. 'They're using a stand-in for the actual fall, so it shouldn't be too difficult.'

'Want to bet? Last time I was involved in anything like that, it took sixteen takes to get it right. Horses know when they've an amateur aboard.'

She hid her trepidation behind the laughter. 'Thanks for the confidence booster!'

'You're welcome.' He added casually, 'Want me to walk you back to your room?'

She shook her head. 'That's something I *can* manage.'

'Yeah.' The inflection was just faintly regretful. 'Happy dreams, honey.'

He was calling for another drink as she left—his third in less than half an hour. His morale booster, he had told her once when she had lightly commented on his capacity for alcohol. Smoothes the rougher edges, he had added drily. She could have stopped him tonight by accepting his offer, Nicola knew, but, the way things had been going lately, she might have found it difficult to leave it there. Dean desperately needed someone in his life. Someone he could trust. Only she wasn't the one to unravel his warped philosophy. It would take love to do that.

She could do with a little unravelling herself, if it came to that, she admitted ruefully. Where Ross was concerned, at least, she was an emotional mess. That she wanted him still was indisputable. He only had to look at her to rouse that ache of longing for all they had once had.

Yet how much had they had, when it all boiled down? Don't change, he had told her, yet she must have finished up boring him, hence his return to Paula Reddington. It was a pretty fruitless exercise, wondering how long they might have gone on if she hadn't found out about Paula. Their marriage was over—dead. It had to be accepted.

Her cabin was one of the better grade at the far end of the rectangle, which meant it had two kingsized instead of queensized beds. Had she been a real star, she thought whimsically, they would have laid on one of those superbly equipped mobile homes for her use while on location. Either that, or flown her in from Dallas for the scenes where she was needed. Not that there were so many where she wasn't. Catherine was the axis around which all the other characters revolved.

Footsteps sounded in her wake, and she stiffened a little, half expecting that Dean had decided to come after her. What did one say, she wondered, to a man one didn't want to hurt?

'Don't look so wary,' said Ross as she turned to glance back. 'My cabin happens to be down this end, too.'

'I thought you were deep in discussion,' she remarked.

'I left them to it.' He fell into step beside her, the white sweater a beacon in the dim light of the walkway. 'I wanted to talk about tomorrow's shoot.'

'What about it?' She was being deliberately obtuse. 'I fall off a horse. Nothing to it!'

'With that attitude, you'll be lucky to survive the first take. The horse you'll be riding won't be any docile stable hack. Think you're capable of handling it long enough to get the close-ups?'

One thing she was not about to do, Nicola thought, was admit to any doubts on that score. 'Of course,' she said. 'After all, I had the best of teachers.' She tagged on recklessly, 'I can handle the fall, too, if you want to dispense with the stand-in.'

'I guess not. An arm or leg in pot wouldn't enhance the characterisation.'

'According to you, the characterisation is lacking anyhow,' she retorted, smarting still at the memory.

'Was,' he corrected. 'As a matter of fact, it was never as bad as I made out. I thought you were in danger of getting too complacent about it, that's all.'

She stopped so suddenly, he was a couple of steps ahead of her before he did likewise. He eyed her steadily. 'Planning on taking another swing?'

Her voice sounded strangled. 'Do you realise what I've been going through this last week? You deliberately set out to undermine every bit of self-confidence I had!'

'No,' he said. 'I knew you well enough to take a chance on your reaction. It worked, too. You've brought Catherine alive.'

Nicola stared at him, her defences in shreds. He was so near, so dear—yes, *dear*. She didn't hate him; she had never hated him. He had hurt her and she had retaliated, the only way she knew how. She didn't want a divorce. She had know that for days. Only it was too late for regrets.

'Aren't you afraid telling me that might make me complacent again?' she got out, and saw him smile a little.

'Not this time.'

'Because I have you to keep my feet on the ground?'

Even in the relative darkness, it was possible to see the sudden spark in his eyes. 'Not tonight, I hope.'

She said thickly, 'You really think I'm so deprived of sex, I'd agree to spending the night with you?'

'Not just the night,' he said. 'I want you back, Nicola.'

Her eyes were dark. 'Until Paula Reddington, or someone like her, made you a better offer.'

'Paula wasn't with me in San Francisco.' He said it quietly. 'There was never any question of her being with me. The reasons I gave for not taking you were genuine.'

Nicola wanted desperately to believe him. Even more desperately, she wanted him to reach out and pull her to him. It had been so long since they had been together.

He must have read the message in her eyes, because he lifted a hand and smoothed the back of it gently down her cheek. 'We've a lot of catching up to do,' he said, 'and a whole night to do it in. Do we take advantage of it?'

Her voice sounded surprisingly calm considering, Nicola thought, except that it wasn't saying what she wanted to say. 'We've an early start in the morning. Shouldn't that take priority?'

The hand fell away, his mouth taking on a slant. 'I guess you're right at that. Set your alarm for five. We can't rely on wake-up calls in this place.'

He had started to move on when she said his name, the sound torn from some deep place over which she had no control. He paused but didn't turn, dark head held at an angle that suggested weariness. 'Yes?'

'I've changed my mind.' She summoned a touch of humour. 'That's a woman's perogative, isn't it?'

'So they tell me.' Ross still didn't look at her. 'As you said, we've an early start in the morning. See you at breakfast.'

She stayed where she was until he had opened the door of his cabin a short distance down the row, and closed it again behind him. There was a taut constriction in her chest. Useless telling herself she had done the right thing. She might not trust Ross, but she still loved him. The knowledge was an ache throughout her whole body. He had made the overture for peace between them and been rejected. It was doubtful whether he would be asking again.

The make-up artist knocked on Nicola's door at five-thirty. At six-fifteen it was the turn of the hairdresser. By seven she ws ready, in full costume, to join the rest of the company on call for breakfast before travelling the few miles out to the site already prepared by the construction crew.

Ross was already seated at table with Rita and Dean. It would look too pointed, Nicola decided, if she ignored the spare chair and joined another group. Her bright 'Good morning,' elicited a sour response from the older woman. Ross simply nodded.

'You'll need more than that to get you through a morning's work,' he stated when she refused the main menu and asked for toast and coffee. 'Bring bacon, two eggs over easy and hash browns,' he told the waitress.

'I can't possibly eat all that!' protested Nicola.

'You can try.' He wasn't giving an inch, his eyes cool and hard as he looked across at her. 'You've lost weight since you were fitted for that jacket. Better get wardrobe to put a tuck in the waist.' He turned his attention back to Rita. 'Where were we?'

'Sleep well?' asked Dean.

Nicola answered without looking up from her coffee. 'Fine, thanks. You?'

'Better than I expected. Three weeks of this place is going to seem like three months!'

Nicola could go along with that sentiment, if for different reasons. She had spent the greater part of the night regretting her over-hasty reaction, yet seeing no way round it. Probably for the best in the long run, she had finished up consoling herself. She needed a deeper, more meaningful relationship than any Ross could offer her. Sitting here now, she knew that was all eyewash. Ross was the man she wanted—the only man she wanted. If he was telling her the truth about Paula, then she had broken up their marriage for nothing. If he was telling her the truth. She still couldn't be sure.

A whole fleet of vehicles drove them out to the film site at eight o'clock, followed by what looked like half the town. The construction crew had done a good job in converting the rented ranch house and outbuildings. Set amid the spreading, empty landscape, it was fronted by a small village of trailers and trucks, with cables running everywhere. The catering wagon staff were already setting out the long trestles from which they would serve a hot luncheon, roping off an area for the folding tables and chairs.

Even thinking about eating again caused Nicola's stomach to stir uneasily. She should have held out against the bacon and eggs, she knew, but it had seemed easier at the time to just go along with it. She was heartily relieved to find it would take an hour or longer to set up the coming scene.

One of the scriptgirls of similar colouring and build was roped in to stand for her while the lighting technicians conferred, leaving her free to retire to the comfortable trailer set aside for her use and study the script she already knew by heart.

The scene called for her to say a few words to the man who had supposedly saddled the horse for her, then mount the animal while he continued to hold its head—although he would be out of camera. With the close-ups in the bag, she would then dismount again, and a professional stand-in would take her place. When the horse started bucking, it would be in long and medium shot, with the rider's face turned away from the camera. The stuntwoman would take the fall, then the cameras would stop rolling once more and she, Nicola, would like down in the dust for more close-ups. It all sounded simple enough on paper, but if past experience was anything to go by it could take all day to get it right.

There was no knock on the door to warn her. Ross closed it again behind him, his expression resolute.

'We're going to sort this out once and for all,' he stated. 'I'm not going to waste any more time trying to convince you about Paula. You believe what you want to believe. Only get this straight. If you want a divorce, you're going to have to fight for it. Name Paula Reddington and I'll name Keir Lawson. Right?'

Nicola stared at him, almost too taken aback by the attack to rally her defenses. 'What does Keir have to do with it?'

'Plenty. He was two days late joining us in Cisco. You met him straight from the airport, didn't you?'

Her eyes darkened. 'Were you having me watched?'

'In our town, honey, there's no need for paid surveillance.' His tone cut like a knife. 'You were seen together not half an hour after you dropped me off.'

She said slowly, 'How long have you known?'

'Does it matter?' He registered a flicker of recollection in her eyes with a slant of a lip. 'I already tackled Lawson about it. He admitted to being in love with you.'

'He isn't in love with me!' The denial broke from stiff lips. 'He hardly knows me. I barely know him!'

'You spent an hour or more watching him make love to your image. That must have given you some insight.'

'*My* image?'

'Sure. He only came alive after you walked on-set that afternoon. You couldn't take your eyes off him, either.'

'There wasn't anywhere else to look!' she retorted

jerkily. 'What is this, Ross? Another attempt to put me in the wrong? I haven't been seeing Keir.'

The grey eyes narrowed. 'You're saying my source was wrong?'

'No.' She saw his mouth tauten again, and made a small, helpless gesture. 'It wasn't an arranged meeting. He just happened to be driving along the same street.'

'Taking a long detour back to the house, were you?'

'So I get lost.' Anger was a saving grace. 'You're writing your own scenario—out of nothing!'

His smile was humourless. 'Circumstantial evidence, it's called. The same stuff you judged me on. Except that I have Lawson's word to back mine up.'

Nicola swallowed on the dryness in her throat. 'What exactly did he tell you?'

'Enough. I beat it out of him.'

'Just like in the films!' she responded with bitter irony. 'Whatever he said, he was doing it to get at you, Ross. Can't you see that? There's never been anything between us.'

He was silent for a long moment, regard steely. 'So we take each other on trust,' he said at last. 'OK?'

'No!' The assumption that she was ready to just put all this behind her lent her a steel of her own. 'I won't stay married to a man who thinks I'm a liar. I'll work with you, because I have to, but I don't want you touching me ever again. OK?'

A dangerous light leapt suddenly in his eyes. There was a matter of several feet between them; he made them seem like inches. Dragged into his arms, feeling the ruthless pressure of his mouth, Nicola tried to keep her lips closed against him, but he was too intent on reaching her to brook any denial.

And he *was* reaching her; she could feel her body trembling, her will-power dwindling, her every sense springing to life. He ran his hands down her back to bring her closer, holding her until she stopped resisting him and started helplessly responding.

The costume she was wearing was not designed to be entered easily, but he managed it, his fingers sliding in to find soft flesh. She closed her eyes as he lowered his head to cover the same spot with his lips, everything else fading from mind but the desire and the need and the love that refused to go away. There was a sofa just behind her. She longed for him to press her down on to it, to strip her of her clothing, to make love to her until they were both too exhausted to fight any more. When he let her go, she couldn't think straight, gazing blindly into the strong, uncompromising features.

Ross was breathing fast himself, but still in control. 'That's the one thing that hasn't changed,' he said. 'We'll use it as a basis. Only not while we're here in this place. It won't do either of us any harm to go without for another three weeks.'

'Ross.' Her voice was low, unsteady. 'It isn't going to work.'

'We can give it another chance.' He turned away from her, tucking his shirt back into his waistband. 'Better get yourself tidied up. They should be ready for you by now.'

Nicola forced her fingers to start refastening the many buttons as he left the trailer. She felt completely at sea. Ross still wanted her, that much was obvious. Yet was it going to be any different once they got back to Los Angeles?

The gathered townsfolk were held back at a distance of several hundred yards when she emerged from the trailer to take her place on set. Even so, she was very much aware of the watching eyes. It was different with the crew because they were all involved in the same job. Having a critical outside audience to witness her efforts certainly made things no easier.

Ross was talking with the man holding the horse's head when she reached her spot after having her make-up checked. He looked her over with what seemed a purely objective eye. 'All set?'

Glancing beyond him to the animal she was to mount, Nicola thought with relief that it seemed quiet enough. She nodded. 'All set?'

'OK, so let's go for a take,' he said, and moved away to where the group of blue-jeaned technicians and sophisticated machinery awaited him.

Waiting for the signal to start, Nicola shut out all thought of the crowd beyond the ropes and willed herself into Catherine's shoes. She heard the clapperboard, followed by 'Action', then she was moving forward to seize hold of the reins, speaking the two short lines as she raised her foot to place it in the stirrup.

Unlike the horse she had ridden in Venezuela, this animal was no more than fifteen hands; it took little real effort to heave herself into the saddle. For a moment, as he moved restlessly beneath her, she felt a stirring of presentiment, then he quietened again and she hastily composed her features for the close-ups. A couple more minutes or so and she would be able to get down.

What happened next was never quite clear. Perhaps the animal sensed her nervousness and reacted to it, or perhaps the man holding his head relaxed both attention and grasp for a moment. Whichever, the sudden rearing took them all by surprise.

Clinging on like grim death to the pommel in front of her, Nicola felt every bone in her body jar as the animal whirled in its tracks and began to buck. Her teeth were coming loose, her head parting from her neck. She felt the stirrups go and tried desperately to cling with her legs, but only for a second or two. When she hit the ground, it was with a thud that drove every ounce of

breath from her body. Lying there, she could hear
voices shouting, the sound of running feet, but she
couldn't summon the energy to move. Then everything
faded.

When she came round again, she was lying on one of
the couches in her trailer, with something wet pressed
to her forehead. She put up a hand to push the wetness
away, and felt it taken in a firm grip. Ross's face came
into view, lean and tense.

'Leave it,' he ordered. 'And lie still. There's a medic
on the way.'

'I'm all right,' she said, and was surprised at the
tinny sound of her voice. 'I passed out, that's all.'

'You *knocked* yourself out. There may be concussion.'

'I'd know if there was.' She came upright, stifling a
groan as her head throbbed. Her smile was only slightly
wavery. 'No harm done. Let's get back on set.'

'It can wait.' His tone was brusque. 'The whole
goddamned film can wait! You're staying right here till
you've been checked out. I don't care how long it
takes.'

'You don't need to stay with me,' she protested. 'You
can shoot round Catherine.'

A faint grim smile touched his lips. 'You trying to tell
me my job?'

'No.' The bravado was fading fast, overshadowed by
the need for comfort, for reassurance, for something to
which she could cling. Her lips still retained a slightly
swollen tenderness from that earlier scene. She touched
them with the tip of her tongue, feeling the tremor like
fingers down her spine. Some things don't change, he
had said. That at least was true. Whether it was enough
on which to rebuild a marriage was something they
would have to find out.

His name came involuntarily as her defences
crumbled, low and shaky and filled with appeal. She

saw his expression alter, his eyes suddenly take on new life. Then he was holding her, his arms warm and strong about her, his lips at her temple.

'I thought I'd lost you,' he said roughly. 'When I saw you lying there, I thought you were dead.'

'Like Arlene?' she whispered, and felt his hold tighten.

'There was no feeling when she died. There never had been much, from either side. We used each other, she and I. You could say we deserved each other. It took a jolt like being arrested to make me realise what I'd become. If you hadn't come along when you did, I'd still be out there in that jungle, wallowing in it.'

'You saved me from a lot worse,' she murmured. 'And let me stay when I needed it.'

'I let you stay because by then I couldn't let you go.' He held her a little away from him so that he could see her face, his own devoid of hardness. 'Have you any idea how much I love you, Nicola?'

'No.' She could hardly get the words out. 'I don't think I do.'

'Then it's time you learned.'

The kiss convinced her. She had never known such tenderness. Clinging to him, she wanted to weep for all the wasted weeks.

'Why didn't you tell me?' she said huskily.

'I did. Or I tried to. It was when we got to LA that things started to go wrong. You seemed to change from the girl I'd known in Venezuela to a stranger I couldn't reach.'

'I was jealous,' she confessed. 'Of your work, of your past, of anything and everything that I wasn't a part of. Thinking you were with Paula in San Francisco was more than I could take.'

'Paula spent the whole of January in Switzerland with some French count,' he said. 'So far as I'm concerned, he's welcome to her.'

Nicola searched the lean features, wanting to believe him. 'Keir said you'd been seen together since you got back.'

'If we did meet, it was inadvertently, not arranged.' He took her face between his hands, looking into her eyes with intensity. 'What do I have to do to convince you? Paula Reddington can't hold a candle to you, in any sphere. You not only make her look like a gilded lily, you can act her into the ground! *Sky* is OK for starters, but the part isn't stretching you. Sam has another property in mind for you. More meat on the bones this time.'

'Isn't it a bit premature to be thinking of using me again before *Sky* is even finished?' she asked. 'Supposing it's a flop?'

'It won't be, if only for the fact that the media are going to make a meal of our relationship. A director who saw off his first wife in order to repeat his Svengali act with another young innocent—that's the conclusion a lot will reach. Think you're going to be able to take it?'

'The only people who really matter will know it isn't true.' Her voice shook a little. 'I love you, Ross. Too much to let outside influences come between us again.'

His kiss revealed an emotion far more telling than words could ever be. 'I owe you so much, my darling. You brought me back to life. The house seemed so empty without you. I wanted to hurt you the way I was hurting.'

'You succeeded,' Nicola admitted. 'Not so much in coming to the apartment that night, but in leaving again the way you did without a word.'

Ross smiled ruefully. 'It was then or never. The only reason I took over direction of *Sky* was because of you. I knew as soon as I saw the rushes that Carl was handling you wrongly. You didn't seem to have any will left of your own. A good stiff jolt was what was needed.'

'And given.' Nicola put up a hand and laid it against the lean, tanned cheek. 'I really excelled myself in the outraged prima donna department, didn't I? You should have hit me right back!'

'Try it again and there's every chance,' he promised.

'Never!' She kissed him long and hard, sensing the desire in him with a sense of exultation in her power to provide. 'We're going to be Hollywood's closest, most compatible couple,' she vowed against his lips, and felt the laugh welling up in his throat.

'We'll probably fight like cat and dog,' he said, 'but the making up will be worth while.'

Fade out to title music, Nicola thought blissfully as he enclosed her securely in his arms.

Harlequin *Presents*

Coming Next Month

Available in February wherever paperback books are sold, or through Harlequin Reader Service.

In the U.S.
901 Fuhrmann Blvd.
P.O. Box 1397
Buffalo, N.Y. 14240-1397

In Canada
P.O. Box 603
Fort Erie, Ontario
L2A 5X3

ATTRACTIVE, SPACE SAVING BOOK RACK

Display your most prized novels on this handsome and sturdy book rack. The hand-rubbed walnut finish will blend into your library decor with quiet elegance, providing a practical organizer for your favorite hard-or soft-covered books.

Only $9.95

Approximately 16" x 8" when assembled

Assembles in seconds!

To order, rush your name, address and zip code, along with a check or money order for $10.70* ($9.95 plus 75¢ postage and handling) payable to *Harlequin Reader Service*:

Harlequin Reader Service
Book Rack Offer
901 Fuhrmann Blvd.
P.O. Box 1396
Buffalo, NY 14269-1396

Offer not available in Canada.

BKR-1A

*New York and Iowa residents add appropriate sales tax

Keepsake

Harlequin Books

You're never too young to enjoy romance. Harlequin for you . . . and Keepsake, young-adult romances destined to win hearts, for your daughter.

Pick one up today and start your daughter on her journey into the wonderful world of romance.

Two new titles to choose from each month.